Hope Rising

BRENDA KILHOFFER

Hope Rising

Paperback ISBN: 979-8-9850673-0-9
Hardcover ISBN: 979-8-9850673-2-3
eBook ISBN: 979-8-9850673-1-6

First Published in the USA in 2021 by Brenda Kilhoffer

Publishing House: Spotlight Publishing™
Chief Editor: Lynn Thompson, Living on Purpose Communications
Book Cover: Angie Ayala
Interior Design: Amit Dey

For Information Contact:
www.CheapMamaLife.com

Hope Rising

Brenda Kilhoffer

Goodyear, AZ

DEDICATION

I dedicate this book to all of the men and women around the world who take a stand for children. While we may disagree on what freedom looks like or how to achieve it, we can find common ground in this simple truth: We want more, better, and different for our children, grandchildren, great-grandchildren, and generations beyond. I've written this book for you, that you may support, guide, and encourage the children entrusted to you to reach their highest purpose. I pray you always focus on what is best for the children and the legacy you will leave behind.

ACKNOWLEDGMENTS

To say I am immensely grateful to all of those who supported me in the evolution of *Hope Rising* is an understatement. From conception to birth, this project spanned eight years, and its contributors are too numerous to acknowledge each and every one.

First and foremost, I give glory to God. He put the inspiration in my heart and guided my head and heart as I worked. He was patient when I put the project on pause, and He spoke clearly when its time arrived.

My husband Rodney truly deserves recognition for his unending support. He encourages and inspires me to dream. He accepts my shortcomings and gives me room to grow. After putting this project on hold for many years to build our business, I stepped away from all money-making activities knowing in my heart that the brand would grow once the book was published. He supported my decisions without question and filled in at home when deadlines approached, and I was up against them. Rodney has been my rock and my biggest fan. He supported our family, and most of all, he loved and supported me.

As you might imagine, there were times I wrote through dinner. I spent time with my publisher or editor on the phone when my children wanted my time and attention. Jaelyn and Jacob took turns making dinner, helped with Jeremiah, and took care of chores and responsibilities they would have preferred mom take care of for them. They are my biggest inspiration, and they hold me accountable for being an excellent example to them. As I chased my dreams, they shared in the sacrifices and witnessed what it takes to go out and pursue their own. Jaelyn and Jacob encouraged me and read countless drafts. Jordan and my daughter-in-love, Lexi, were a big part of the launch. And Jeremiah remains my biggest fan. He loves me when we fall behind at home school because I was involved in edits and then works his little tail off to catch up. He gives me hugs and energy every day and has even set out to write his own book!

My publisher, Becky Norwood, is quite simply a saint. She rolled with the punches, extended deadlines and supported me 100% when I called and said, "I know I said I was rewriting (it's a surprise), but I really feel like *Hope Rising* is the book I need to write right now." She's been a guiding light through this experience. She has patiently supported me over the past year, provided me with referrals for editors, guidance for everything from writing to listening to my book, and worked tirelessly behind the scenes to create a beautiful cover, layout, and a successful launch.

My hero, my saving grace, in this project was Lynn Thompson, my editor. Throughout my journey, I've learned to set deadlines on goals. My deadline was less than a week away when I reached out to Lynn, yet she took on this project and dove all in. She worked tirelessly and helped to create nothing short of a miracle. She took on additional pieces of the project outside of her contractual obligation and truly supported me. I am genuinely grateful to have found a kindred soul who is truly as passionate about my project as I am.

Finally, I am grateful to all of those who've taught me the lessons that show up throughout Natazhia's experiences. As much as I wish to acknowledge each and every one of you, I'm sure I'd leave someone out. The reality is every single person I've crossed paths with has made me the person I am today. Therefore, you helped to shape and give dimension to the characters and the situations they experienced that you read about in *Hope Rising.*

Brenda Kilhoffer

FOREWORD

Our connection was instant when I met Brenda Kilhoffer on the Transform U Media Network in early 2021. As we continue to build on our relationship, both personally and professionally, I am doing what I enjoy most in my life, supporting another amazing woman who has stepped into greatness. Brenda is one of the most gifted women I know. Although we have not met in person yet, her spirit is connected with mine as if we met years ago.

There are three reasons that I welcomed Brenda's request to be on the *Hope Rising* launch team. First, since that day I met the author, she has been willing to share her expertise and dreams with me. Being a professional mentor, it takes courage for someone to trust me with the intimacy of her aspirations. Brenda has shown a level of trust and resilience that transcends the ordinary. Second, when Brenda and I connected on the network, we immediately began a professional collaborative relationship. Brenda said to me, "I want to be a part of whatever you are a part of." As a professional woman, connecting with women who support my vision is priceless. Third, learning more about Brenda's character through the words of *Hope Rising* draws forth my desire to learn more about her hidden talents that I know will manifest after the launch of this epic tale.

In many ways, I believe that the storyline of *Hope Rising* gives the reader a glimpse into the highs and lows of Brenda's experiences with leadership. The way the characters play out through the pages, the reader feels present for all the action, learning alongside them in the face of opposition and circumstance.

This book will take you on a ride of adventure, suspense, and even some emotional cycles of happiness and disappointment. So, settle into your quiet place with your warm drink and blanket. It's time to nestle into *Hope Rising!*

Anntricia Bray Smith
Professional Mentor and Speaker
Author of *Recreating A Better Me, Struggling To Forgive,* and *Financial Education Simplified.* Founder of Christian Women Fellowship (Education Institution), and Initiative for Marketing Success Alliance (Professional Development Alliance).

TABLE OF CONTENTS

1

HIDING OUT

Natazhia gently pulled the door to her daughter's room halfway closed after giving her a good night hug and kiss. She smiled to herself, grateful that her 14-year-old daughter, Serenity, still welcomed prayers, hugs, and kisses at bedtime, then walked down the hall to the boys' bedroom. Natazhia wasn't at all surprised to find them out of bed and their room in total disarray.

"Blaise! Jacob!" she said with the sternest voice she could muster up, trying to hide the laughter and joy she felt watching the twins play with one another. "It's already past bedtime! I want you to pick this room up right now! You've got two minutes!"

Natazhia turned and walked toward the living room to call her husband, Ryker, for reinforcement. Despite Natazhia's strong and sometimes intimidating personality, her children, especially the boys, walked all over her.

Ryker Flynn was a gentle and quiet man. At six foot four with a muscular build, there was strength in his calm demeanor, and the boys usually did as their father asked. Natazhia had met Ryker more than twenty years earlier at a rodeo in the formerly booming city of Phoenix, Arizona. Unlike the city, he hadn't changed much over the years, except now gray and white hair peppered the sandy blond hair, showing his age.

"Ryker," she called, walking through the kitchen to the living room to find him, "I could use some help with your boys." She found him where he often was found, sitting at her late mother's antique desk scanning the computer for news of rebellion skirmishes.

Natazhia melted as Ryker turned to look at her with those hazel eyes, a window to his heart, showing his obvious amusement despite his otherwise poker face. It had been Ryker's eyes that attracted Natazhia so many years earlier, and even now, as he got up and walked toward her.

The couple left Phoenix after the Federal Government took control of the water supply from the Colorado River to punish the vast majority of citizens who had formed a rebellion to secede from the United States when the Government repealed the Second Amendment. They had been among those fortunate enough to own and occupy the family's former vacation home (thanks to Natazhia's mother, Eyleen) well off the beaten track near Oak Creek in Sedona. Most of the rebels occupied abandoned houses. There had been no routes out of Arizona after the former state had been surrounded with armed guards to ensure weapons did not leave the Liberation. At Eyleen's prodding, they had stocked the vacation home with a year's worth of food as well as solar power and its own well. They were grateful that solar had become the norm prior to the Liberation takeover that was a by-product of the increasingly restrictive climate control laws. Otherwise, they wouldn't be able to enjoy the household amenities that required power. With the other refugees, they had formed a tight-knit community that remained entirely off the grid and undiscovered by most of the Rebellion Leaders and the Reformed Liberation of America.

Natazhia giggled to herself as she listened to Ryker lecturing the boys about their bedtime, and heard him say, "Jacob, get in that bed right now!"

"Daaaddd!" Jacob shrieked. "I don't have my homework in my backpack! And it's all 'cause you didn't sign it! And I can't find my school shoes!"

Ryker laughed. "It's a wonder you boys can find anything in this mess!"

Natazhia recognized Jacob's high-pitched squeal and knew he was about to reach his boiling point. The last thing they needed at this hour was for Jacob to lose his temper.

Most of the time, Jacob was sweet, gentle, and thoughtful. Natazhia adored the older of the twins, and he was her favorite to cuddle. Her eyes scanned the mess in the room before resting them upon Blaise sitting on the top bunk. It took only a second to see by the look on his face that he was the source of Jacob's frustration.

"Blaise," she said, questioning the younger twin, "do you know where Jacob's shoes are?"

"Uhhhh, maybe." He grinned sheepishly.

"Well," Natazhia looked sternly up at her son, "I'd suggest you get right down here and get your brother's shoes."

Blaise jumped off the top bunk, and at the exact moment, his parents yelled. "Blaise, NO!"

Ryker was clearly frustrated with the unfolding scene. "You know better than to jump off of that bed! We don't need any more scars! Besides, if you seriously hurt yourself, you don't understand how difficult it is to get around all of the Rebellion skirmishes to get help! Do you want to see your mom or I get captured, or worse? You've gotta think, boy!"

Blaise, who loved to be the center of attention, hopped across the room and dove under the pile of dirty clothes in the corner of their space to retrieve Jacob's shoes. Standing up with both shoes in his hands, he exclaimed, "Ta-Da! They were right here the whole time! All he had to do was open his eyes!"

Natazhia folded her arms across her chest. "Blaise, you know as well as I do that your brother is very particular about where he puts his things. He wouldn't have to look for them if someone hadn't buried them under his dirty clothes!" Turning to leave the room, she said, "All right, dudes, I'll be right back for kisses and prayers, and I expected you both to be in bed and tucked in!"

Natazhia looked at the clock when she walked back into the kitchen. She had a lot of work yet to prepare for the following day. The twins and their bedtime stall tactics cut into the valuable time she needed for preparation. Sitting down at the kitchen table with a pen and paper, she began to make a list of all of the items she would need to find at the trading post the following day.

Lye

Cinnamon

Olive Oil

Coconut Oil

Lavender Oil

Flour

Thread

Fabric

Corn Meal

There were lots of items left to pack for the trip to the trading post. Natazhia had to gather eggs, jerky, and quilts, as well as a few of her handmade soaps and candles. Few citizens had the survival skills Natazhia's parents had taught her and her brothers when they were growing up. Fewer had ever learned any of the lost arts. Her mom had taught her how to make soaps, candles, and quilts when she was a young girl. Natazhia had never imagined these skills would be critical to her family's survival. And now, because of the Liberation's trade restrictions, it was tough for anyone in the region to find even basic necessities they had taken for granted back in 2021. Due to their rarity, Natazhia's soaps and quilts were prized and always resulted in more provision than she required to reinvest in making the new batch for the next trading post quarter.

Natazhia stood up, glad to be done with the list, stretched, and went in to check on her boys. Both were in bed waiting for her kisses. She stepped on the ladder to reach Blaise on his top bunk and gave him a kiss on the cheek, and traced the sign of the cross over his forehead. Then she kneeled down next to Jacob's bed and began to give him ten kisses on his cheek.

"Slowly, Mom!" he whined.

"I am going slow, Jacob," Natazhia replied.

"I want fifteen then, on each side!"

Natazhia smiled. "And tomorrow you'll want twenty. I love you, now get some sleep." She also traced his forehead with the sign of the cross.

As Natazhia stood up and left their children's room, she reflected on her childhood life. *Oh, how I miss going to Church each week. I would give anything for my children to experience a Sunday morning service just like I used to. They have no idea of the freedoms this new world denies them.*

Ryker came from behind and placed his hand reassuringly on her shoulder. "I know, honey. I miss it too!"

Startled, she asked, "What are you talking about?"

"Church, of course! Isn't that what you're thinking about? I saw you with the boys."

Natazhia looked up at Ryker. "You know me too well." She smiled and placed her hand on his chest, pushing gently. "Come on, let's get everything packed up for tomorrow."

Natazhia hated leaving the children those times when both she and Ryker went for supplies at the trading post; however, it was far too dangerous to take them along. In the past, until recently, Ryker went with Mr. Johnson and the women stayed behind with the children. On those occasions when Natazhia and Ryker went together, Serenity was usually home with the twins. This trek would be the first time for leaving one of the twins by himself when they were away for the day.

She and Ryker were violating the two-child limit that had been enforced long before the twins were born. The Chinese had limited the population of their citizens when she was a child. Natazhia never imagined it would also be the case in America. Her mother, having fought so hard to repeal abortion laws when she was alive, would be so angered that now they weren't only legal; they were forced upon the citizens. Even in her small community, Natazhia kept the twins a secret. Only one of the boys went to school each day with his sister, and they traded off regularly. Blaise and Jacob were completely identical. The only distinguishing features were Blaise's small dark birthmark just a little bit bigger than a freckle on his right jawline and the small scar along the top of his left eyebrow. Natazhia found his birthmark endearing because it reminded her of her mother, who had the same birthmark on her jawline. The scar, further evidence of Blaise's unlimited energy, occurred when he jumped off of the living room table at the age of two.

Survival wasn't easy, especially in Rebel Territory. Natazhia and Ryker would not turn themselves into the Liberation, despite hearing that the Liberation took good care of those living under the strict rules. If they gave themselves over, one of the twins would likely be executed, and if by God's grace were allowed to live, he would never be entitled to the rights of legal children. Besides, she and Ryker would be severely punished for not terminating one of them early in the pregnancy. As the children's parents, if they were imprisoned or, worse, put to death, Natazhia refused to allow herself to think about all that could happen to Serenity, Jacob, and Blaise without their protection.

When Serenity was seven and Natazhia suspected she was pregnant again, she had traveled the distance to Phoenix to see her mother's trusted friend and doctor, Dr. Shavilla. He had fought alongside her mother to end abortion and had been with her through two miscarriages. Natazhia trusted Dr. Shavilla. The Liberation mandate that no woman could have more than two children further stated that one child had to be male and the other female. Liberation Doctors were required by law to terminate any pregnancy that exceeded a woman's legal child limit regardless of how late in term the pregnancy had become. Natazhia had a nagging feeling that her pregnancy did not meet the guidelines and knew Dr. Shavilla would not force her to terminate the pregnancy if the ultrasound revealed she was carrying a daughter. She had never considered the news Dr. Shavilla shared, when he soon determined that Natazhia was pregnant with twin boys. He urged her to return to their wooded retreat in Sedona quickly and not to leave her home after the 28th week of pregnancy when she would be showing. He agreed to visit during the last trimester to deliver the babies. True to his word, Dr. Shavilla saw Natazhia through a difficult third trimester and delivery. She couldn't imagine a life without the twins.

Despite all of the fears of leaving the children at home on their own, Natazhia knew that, for their family's survival, she and Ryker had to make the two-hour trek to the trading post. To prepare for leaving the next morning, the couple went out the back door into the evening light and followed the flagstone trail to the storage shed behind the garden. After unlocking and opening the shed, Ryker stepped in, followed by Natazhia who locked the shed door from the inside. And then together, they pushed the sparsely-stocked set of shelves away from the middle of the room. The modest supply of canned vegetables and beef jerky on those shelves were for daily use and displayed as a decoy of poverty if they were ever discovered or raided by looters. Their treasure of supplies and defense was hidden below, and Ryker continued with their routine to access it. Rolling away the thick rubber insulating mat from the floor revealed two hinged wooden cellar doors that once opened, exposed the heavy steel door with a combination deadbolt. Ryker quickly typed in the code and lifted the heavy steel door to their underground storage cellar. Built in preparation for the need to live off the grid while Natazhia's mother was still alive, Ryker had reinforced the entire basement cellar with steel and welded all of its joints, making it impossible for the average looter to access.

Natazhia followed her husband down the ladder into the cellar with her Browning .380 caliber pistol strapped to her leg, and knowing that Ryker had his Colt 45 on his hip, Natazhia hated that her children lived in a world where their parents carried their guns with them at all times. At the same time, she knew how blessed she had been to live in Arizona when the Liberation began to take weapons away from its citizens. Before the Libertarian Revolution, Arizona had been one of the states with the least restrictive gun control laws. As the United States began stripping its citizens of religious freedoms and restricting some weapons, Natazhia's parents began storing their family's old hunting rifles and handguns they'd collected for sport over the years. Her father, Charles, who had worked in commercial construction in Phoenix when the city was a booming Metropolis, had worked side by side with Ryker to build the underground storage unit at his and Eyleen's summer home. These days, besides food storage, Natazhia and Ryker had a small arsenal of rifles and ammunition below ground. It always made Natazhia nervous that someone might follow them through the shed into the cellar and attempt to overtake their stockpile. However, she was comforted that her husband was still alive, unlike the husbands of many of the women living in "refugee territories" like Arizona.

On their trek to the trading post the next day, the couple would only be able to carry their backpacks and a small trunk tied with rope on the three-wheeler they had kept together all of these years with scraps Ryker held onto from Charles' and his late father's garages. Choosing carefully what she had room to take, Natazhia pulled out bags of dried parsley, mustard, and peppers, as well as some seeds she had collected from her tomatoes over the spring. She also had eggs from her chickens that she had preserved with mineral oil, along with canned tomatoes, pickles, pumpkin, okra from the garden, and apricots from their trees. Ryker stocked up on ammunition and grabbed the only semi-automatic rifle they had. Natazhia's father bought it shortly after a school shooting back in 2012. At the time, media coverage and public outrage over the lack of gun control made it clear to Charles that if he didn't buy a semi-automatic soon, new restrictions would prohibit him from owning one. Eyleen was beside herself when Charles bought it.

Natazhia could still recall their argument. "What on earth are you going to do with that thing?" That night, when she heard her mother yelling, Natazhia was already in bed. She listened intently.

"I don't know. I've just always thought it would be cool to have one. You never know; I may need it to protect my family someday." As Natazhia thought about her dad, she could picture his twinkling eyes smiling at her mother, even as she was outraged at his decision.

Her mother had replied angrily, "Well, you need to get a safe or somewhere to store it. The last thing I want is to lose a child because one of them thinks it's a toy!"

At the time, Natazhia sided with her mother, hating the idea of guns and people being killed, but tonight she breathed a sigh of relief as her husband placed the rifle alongside their packs to carry upstairs for their trip.

"I still remember when Daddy bought that thing. Mom was so mad," she said, not really expecting a response from Ryker.

"I bet! Your mom probably made him suffer for weeks." Ryker chuckled.

"Oh, yeah. Mother sure did. But I'm happy that was one of the things he stood his ground on."

"You really miss them, don't you, honey?" Ryker asked, pushing her light brown hair away from her face as her bright blue eyes appeared to well up with tears.

"She died living her purpose and for a good cause," Natazhia said hastily, turning away so as not to let Ryker see her vulnerability. Despite the years of hearing her mother talk about how vulnerability is a good thing and even necessary in a relationship, the years of living in hiding, fighting for their lives and freedom, had hardened Natazhia. Even at his tenderest, she refused to be vulnerable in front of her husband.

"Let's get these packs upstairs and get some sleep, Mr. Flynn. We've got a long day ahead of us!" She grabbed the smaller of the two packs and headed up the ladder.

Shaking his head and left wondering what he'd done wrong, Ryker followed. "You're right, babe. And I'm not looking forward to it! I'll close up. Will you take a look outside to be sure no one is out there?"

After looking out into the woods through the small windows on all four sides of the shed, Natazhia said, "It's all clear, hon!" just as Ryker appeared at the top of the ladder with the semi-automatic and the other backpack.

Ryker locked up the steel door, and then closed the wooden cellar doors over it. Natazhia left her pack by the shed door and after Ryker rolled out the heavy gray mat, together, they pushed the shelves back into place in the middle of the shed to disguise their secret underground entrance. Natazhia turned out the shed light and they both peeked out the small windows before exiting. Ryker locked the shed door while Natazhia kept watch, and when he had it secured, they walked hand in hand back to the main house, Ryker pulling a wagon full of the items they had gathered.

After placing everything on the kitchen counter, Natazhia went to her craft room and gathered five pounds of lavender soap she had made with lye, coconut, lavender, and olive oils. She looked over at the quilts she had just finished and picked two of them to take. Her quilts always brought more than the fair market at the trading post. She remembered the first quilt her mother had made back when Natazhia was in third grade. Everything had been so simple then. It seemed so long ago, that time her mother made a quilt to auction off at a fancy fundraiser for her school. Today, she made quilts out of necessity. There were no schools for fundraisers, just a small community gathering children in a nearby barn to teach them basic survival, hunting, weapons training, self-defense, reading, writing, computers, and surveillance. It didn't seem possible that things had changed so much in only 28 years. *If Mom hadn't decided to make that quilt, I'd never have learned this skill.* She looked up and barely whispered, "Thanks, Mom!"

Natazhia took her crafts out to the kitchen, stuffed them in packs, grabbed a glass of water, and walked down the hall to the couple's bedroom.

"Which of the boys is going to school tomorrow?" Ryker asked when she walked into the room.

Instinctively, Natazhia reached for her pistol, then realized it was her husband. He had startled her. She had not realized he was already in bed. Relaxing a bit, she said, "Jacob. Don't you remember his little meltdown over his school shoes?" She sat down on the bed and began unstrapping the pistol from her leg, setting it gently on the nightstand.

"Oh, yes, that's right." He laughed. "I will go over surveillance in the morning and set Blaise up with the emergency radio."

Standing up to remove her jeans, Natazhia asked, "Do you really think we should let Serenity and Jacob go to school tomorrow? What if they all just stayed home? I hate the idea of Blaise here all by himself."

Ryker's voice softened. "I know, honey. I've gone through all of it in my mind too. But you know how the neighbors check in when either of the children misses school. They know we are going to the trading post, and all would agree the children are safer at school with the protection offered there than home alone. If Serenity and Jacob aren't at school, I'm afraid someone would come by our compound to check on them. I just don't trust the others not to turn us in for their own gain if they discover Blaise and Jacob together."

"I know, Ryker. But he's only six, he's just a baby. I hate the idea of leaving him here by himself." She pulled her flannel pajamas up and crawled into bed. "I just wish there were another way."

Ryker reached over and tousled her hair. "I know, babe, these kids are much more prepared for the world than we were at their age. They've had to be. Blaise will be just fine."

Natazhia sighed. "Well, I hope he doesn't get into too much mischief!" She leaned over, kissed Ryker on the cheek, and said, "Good night, let's get some sleep; it's going to be a long day tomorrow." She rolled over and fell asleep almost immediately.

2

RESISTANCE

The sun shone through the bedroom window over Natazhia's pillow. The brightness startled her, and she jumped, waking Ryker as she reached over him for the wind-up alarm clock on his side of the bed.

"What? What? Is something wrong?" he asked groggily as he too, startled.

"The alarm didn't go off, Ryker! I don't hear the kids up! We can't get a late start on a trading post day! The inventory will all be gone!"

Rolling over, Ryker reached for the clock and said, "It hasn't gone off because it's only 5:00 am. Relax, we still have forty-five minutes before we need to wake up the kids! Besides, we can't leave for the trading post until we've dropped Serenity and Jacob off at school."

Her heart racing, Natazhia laid back down, and she tried to fall back asleep. It was too late; her mind was reeling with thoughts of all the preparation for the trip out of Sedona to the old mining-then-turned-tourist town, once known as Jerome, which now served as a trading post for Rebellion Forces and Refugees who lived in the high desert. The thirty-eight-mile trek from their home to the trading post would take a couple of hours on the three-wheel all-terrain vehicle (ATV), provided they didn't run into any trouble. Natazhia could visualize every twist and turn, and as she lay there, sleepless, her mind wandered to all of the possible scenarios that could unfold. *What you resist persists!* she reminded herself. *What you focus on expands!*

Convinced there was no chance of sleep, Natazhia sat up, turned the old wooden nightstand so that its back faced her, and slid her hand underneath it, pulling on the hidden drawer. She drew out a worn and tattered Bible and worn leather-bound devotional, wrapped together carefully in a piece of cloth. Her mother had given her the Bible and devotional when Serenity was born. The fabric covering the Bible was the blanket that her mother wrapped her brother Jonathan in after being delivered, stillborn at only 18 weeks. Natazhia carefully removed the books from their protective cover then flipped through the pages to September 23rd, *Surrender. Control is but an illusion that separates you from Him. You have no control when you release control of that; you create space in your heart for His gifts to dwell and strengthen within. You become an instrument of His will, doing His good works.* At the bottom of the page, the author suggested Psalm 46 for further reading. Natazhia reached for her Bible and opened to Psalm 46. Toward the end of the prescribed lesson, she read the words, *Be still and know that I am God!* After sitting on the edge of the bed for a few more moments, allowing the words from the devotional and her Bible to settle into her heart, she wrapped the old piece of cloth around the precious volumes. She placed her hand lovingly over the fabric for a moment, then reached back down below the nightstand and returned them to the hidden drawer.

She hesitated a moment. *I should take these with me.* Instead of retrieving them, though, she closed the drawer. *It's too risky. There's no place to hide them if we get searched. They are safe here, and we'll be back tonight.* Natazhia walked over to the bathroom, opened the cupboard below the sink, pulled her only brush out of the basket, and began brushing her long hair.

"Why don't you come back in here and get some more rest before the kids get up and demand breakfast?" Ryker called.

"I can't sleep," said Natazhia.

"Have you even tried?"

Agitated by his reply, Natazhia snapped back. "My mind is racing. I can't help but worry about the boys. What if Blaise leaves the house and someone finds him? What if something happens to us?"

Ryker sighed. "I didn't mean to upset you, honey. I'm just worried that you haven't had enough sleep. We are going on a hard, rough ride, and I need you to be on your A-game. I'm just thinking of you!"

Her voice softened. "I know, babe. I just hate leaving them."

Ryker said, "I know, so do I. Believe me, so do I." After a long pause, he went on. "Tell me, what message did God have in store for you this morning?"

Laughing, Natazhia said, "That I should let go of control."

Ryker laughed too. "Well, I think He's going to have to hit you over the head with that one for it to sink in!"

"Shut up!" Walking over to the closet, Natazhia said out loud without expecting an answer, "I wonder how cold it is today, if I need my jacket." She rummaged through the closet, looking for a pair of her mother's old camouflaged pants. She had found the box of her mother's Air Force uniforms in the attic recently while Ryker placed small access doors throughout the house that lead to the attic and their additional stash of rifles and shotguns. The dark green woodland camouflage provided a sense of comfort and security nothing else seemed to provide on trading post days. It wasn't that they afforded much in the way of disguise. More so, she felt her mom was with her on the treacherous roads between their compound and the trading post. "Yes! I found them!" Natazhia exclaimed. Still standing in her closet, she pulled on her mother's pants, then reached for a creamy beige sweater and pulled it over her T-shirt. The late September weather was pretty unpredictable in the high desert. She walked from the closet back into her bathroom and began lathering her face with coconut oil and zinc she had traded for a quilt when they were at the trading post in June. It was rare to find luxuries like sunblock, lotions, and perfumes at the trading post. When they were available, they were costly. Ryker didn't trust such items as typically, they come from Liberation soldiers. He suspected someone could cause harm by mixing chemicals into the perfumes. Natazhia's zinc and coconut oil mixture would have to suffice for protection from the sun.

Satisfied that she was ready for the day, Natazhia went to the kitchen to prepare breakfast. It had become a Flynn family tradition to prepare a big breakfast on trading post days. While Ryker and Natazhia made it a point to eat dinner every night with their children, breakfasts were usually nothing more than powdered protein shakes from their emergency food storage kits. Trading post days were different. It was essential to both Natazhia and Ryker that the family have a large meal together before leaving. That way, if anything were to happen to them, the children would have spent quality time over a feast with their parents as one of their last memories of being together.

Natazhia pulled out eggs and sausage from the deer meat Ryker had brought home on his last hunting trip, flour, and rice. *What I wouldn't give for potatoes,* she thought, looking at the rice as she poured it into the rice cooker with several cups of water. Along with the fridge and the old stove, it was one of the few kitchen appliances that still worked. Catching herself, she said out loud, "Praise you, Jesus, for the stores of rice we have and for keeping it dry and bug-free all of these years." After mixing the flour with some buttermilk courtesy of Hattie, her oldest goat, Natazhia began cooking the sausage and heating oil on the stove to make the children's favorite pancakes. Looking over at the old-fashioned cuckoo clock on the wall, she thought to herself, *and I'd better make sure everyone else is up.*

"Ryker! Ryker!" she called, "Ryker, are you up?"

Still groggy from sleep, Ryker stumbled into the kitchen. "Yeah, babe. I'm up. What do you need?"

"Well, which do you want? Pancakes or waking up the kids?" she asked, smiling and handing the spatula over to him.

"Oh, no." He smiled, hands up, saying no to the spatula. "I'm not cooking today. Besides, it looks like you're doing just fine in here without me. I'll go wake up the kids."

Before she could object, Ryker retreated down the hall to the twins' bedroom. Natazhia continued tending to the pancakes and sausage, then began cracking and plopping eggs into a glass bowl. Natazhia hoped the chicks born this past spring would produce as many eggs as her old hen, Agatha. Eggs came in handy for cooking and trading, and she wasn't sure Agatha and the rest of the flock would continue to keep up with the demand for much longer.

It wasn't long before Ryker and the children joined her in the kitchen.

"Mom," said Jacob, as he grabbed a step stool from the pantry and pulled it up beside her at the stove, "don't forget to make me an inchworm!"

"Grow up, Jacob. They all taste the same," Serenity said, arguing with her brother.

"Do you want Mom to make you a butterfly, sweetheart?" Ryker teased.

"No, I gave that up a long time ago, Dad!" Serenity replied indignantly.

"I want a giant sea squid, Mom!" Blaise shouted.

"Ssshh, son, we're all right here," said Ryker.

"A giant sea squid?" Natazhia laughed. "I will do my best to accommodate. I'm just not sure I know how to make a sea squid-shaped pancake."

The Flynns bantered back and forth as Natazhia finished making breakfast. The children knew the danger their parents faced all too well once they finished breakfast and the children went to school. But for the moment, they were all too happy to enjoy one another and pretend the day ahead didn't exist.

"Okay, Blaise," Natazhia said, pleased that the children were learning to contribute, "it's time to set the table. Jacob, can you get drinks?"

Jacob replied, "Sure, Mom. Do we get to have milk today?"

Natazhia answered her son with a smile. "Yes, I just put some of Hattie's fresh milk in the refrigerator in the garage yesterday." Natazhia smiled even more when she heard his excited whisper as he ran out of the kitchen.

"Yeesss!" He disappeared down the hall toward the garage to fetch the prized milk.

"Mom," Serenity asked quietly, "is there anything I can do?"

Natazhia hugged her daughter and said, "Of course, sweetie. I would love it if you could come over here and help me serve up the plates."

Once they had all of the plates, silverware, and drinks on the table, the family gathered around.

"Let's say grace," said Ryker.

Together the family recited a prayer their grandmother had taught them. "Bless us O' Lord, for these thy gifts which we are about to receive through the bounty of Christ, our Lord. Amen."

Ryker finished, saying, "Lord, only you know what this day will bring. We ask that you watch over each member of our family, keep us safe, and open our hearts and ears that we may hear your voice today and the wisdom and courage to do your will. We ask this in the name of your son, Jesus Christ. Amen."

Together, Natazhia and the children said, "Amen."

An eerie silence fell over the table as everyone began eating. Natazhia knew Ryker's words were on all their minds. Trading post days always caused anxiety for the Flynns. Families in the community had lost loved ones as they traveled to and from the trading post. They had also heard of refugees in other towns whose homes were robbed and looted by thieves who expected to find them empty. The latter concerned Natazhia and Ryker more than their safety. Ryker was a good shot, and Natazhia could undoubtedly handle her own. They weren't sure their six-year-old son, Blaise, had it in him to shoot and kill a trespasser, despite all of the training they had done with the children. If he did have to fire a weapon, one of the neighbors who stayed behind would indeed investigate, despite their remote location. The thought that someone might discover their secret scared Natazhia more than anything.

It was times like these when Natazhia wondered if she had done the right thing. Her mother had instilled in her a belief that all human life was valuable and should be protected. Even still, would it have been more humane to obey the law and allow Liberation doctors to abort one of her twins than to put them through all of the stress of keeping their existence a secret? They shared a single birth certificate. As far as the world was concerned, they shared one identity. *Oh God, in my heart, I know I did the right thing by you. Did I do what was best for these children? Please protect them today and always.* She wiped a tear from her eye and picked up her plate. Placing it in the sink she turned to look at her family, savoring the sight of them sitting together at the table for one more moment. "All right, gang. It's time for school. Get your books, and I'll walk you over to the Johnsons' barn," she said, then turned to the sink again so the children wouldn't see the tears she was holding back.

Serenity and Jacob took their plates to the sink and retreated to their rooms to retrieve their school supplies.

"I'll clean up the kitchen and get Blaise settled in while you're gone," offered Ryker.

"Thank you. I won't be too long," Natazhia promised.

Serenity and Jacob approached the kitchen, each with a backpack and bow and arrows tossed casually over their shoulders.

"Come on over, you two, and give me a hug and kiss," Ryker said. Serenity and Jacob rushed over to their father and clung to him, both doing their best not to show any fear. "I love you guys, too. No worries, we'll be back by the time you go to bed. I promise."

His son and daughter held on to him a few moments longer before letting go and turning, ready to leave with their mother, who was tightening the last strap of the holster for her .380 to her leg.

Natazhia grabbed her leather jacket she had flung over the chair the night before and pulled it over her sweater. She loved the feel and weight of the soft, worn coat that fit her perfectly after years of wear and conditioning. "All right, kiddos, let's go. We don't want to be late for today's lessons." Natazhia shoved her hands in her jacket pocket as they stepped outside into the cool morning air. The sun was warm on her face, and instinctively she knew that it would be a beautiful day.

Serenity and Jacob followed her as she walked along the east edge of the garden.

She stopped briefly at the chicken coops to pour more feed into the feed trough. "Agatha, don't you eat all that yourself, share it with Alfred, the girls, and babies!"

Serenity giggled. "Mom, you don't seriously think that old hen listens to you!"

Natazhia joked back. "I think that sometimes, old Agatha listens better than you children." She put her arm around Serenity's shoulder and gave it a good squeeze.

"Mom," said Jacob, "I listen to you."

Laughing, she pulled Jacob close with her free arm and said, "Of course you do, sweetie."

The three of them walked together for a few moments, Serenity tucked under one arm, and Jacob tucked under the other. No one said a word.

When they reached the gate at the edge of their compound, Natazhia pulled her arms loose, fumbled around in her pockets, and found the key to the wrought iron security gate reinforced with barbed wire. Before opening the gate, she looked around at the perimeter of her property and the Johnsons' adjacent property to ensure no intruders were waiting for an opportunity. Seeing no one, she carefully opened the gate enough for each of the children to squeeze through with their backpacks and bows and arrows. She followed them, then closed and locked the gate. They crossed a narrow dirt road then ducked under a grove of blackberry bushes, being careful not to scratch themselves on its sharp spines. Once on the other side of the bushes, they were able to walk along the fence line of Mr. and Mrs. Johnson's property. Like their own, it was almost unnoticeable behind the trees and bushes—walking between the bushes and the fence line made strangers less likely to notice the well-used path between the properties.

Letty Johnson's mother had been a college professor and homeschooled her daughter. Letty was one of the few residents in their small community with a higher level of education. While Natazhia and Ryker had attended private schools as children, the colleges in Arizona had all but closed their doors when the state began to rebel against the Libertarian Reform. Like many of their neighbors, the couple heeded their parents' warnings and remained in Arizona when they graduated from high school. Letty's mother continued to educate her daughter in business, arts, and sciences at the college level. The Johnson compound was relatively central to most of the neighboring compounds. Her educational background and location made their barn the perfect schoolhouse.

"Mom," Jacob said, "what time will you and Dad be back tonight?"

Natazhia knew she had to answer carefully. She didn't want to worry her son, and she didn't want to make a promise she couldn't keep. "Daddy and I will do everything we can to be home before you go to bed tonight, honey."

Jacob wasn't satisfied with her answer. "But what if you're not?"

Natazhia tried to reassure him. "If we're not, just know that we are doing everything we possibly can to get back home to you as quick as we can."

Still unconvinced, Jacob continued. "But Mom, who's going to feed us and walk us to school, and tell me what days it's my turn to go to school if you're not back tonight?"

Serenity reassured her brother. "I will, Jacob, don't worry. Mommy's taught me everything I need to know to take care of you and Blaise. We'll be okay until they get home. I promise."

Breathing a sigh of relief, Natazhia said, "See, buddy? Nothing to worry about, your sister's got it all figured out. Besides, it's going to take all-out war to keep Mommy and Daddy away from you guys."

They were rounding the corner of the Johnsons' property. Letty was standing by the gate, waiting for all of the students to arrive.

"We'll keep a close eye on the kids, Natazhia. Jasper is planning to walk them home this afternoon when school is over. I can make sure he clears the house for them and—"

"Oh no, Letty," Natazhia said quickly, "I mean, I adore your son, but both he and Serenity are getting older—"

Letty had a puzzled look on her face. "They wouldn't—"

"—Oh, I know, I don't think they would either, but I don't want to make allowances for boys to be in our home under any circumstances, if you know what I mean."

Letty smiled. "Of course, I understand. I would feel the same way if she were my daughter. Very well, I will have him take them to the gate, get them inside your compound, and ensure it is locked up. No further."

Relieved, Natazhia said, "Thank you, Letty. I appreciate you."

Natazhia turned to her children and hugged them tightly. "Be good at school today. When you get home, stay put. We will be there before you know it."

Serenity whispered in her mother's ear. "Please be careful, Mom. I love you. And if anything happens—"

Natazhia shook her head. "No, we can't think that way, and nothing will happen." She held her daughter's face and looked into her eyes.

"I know, Mom; I just want you to know you can count on me."

Natazhia said, "I know I can, baby." Then she kissed her daughter on the cheek and hugged her one last time. Bending down on one knee, she looked into Jacob's eyes and said, "You, buddy, take good care of your brother and sister. Make sure they cook a good dinner tonight, okay?"

Jacob smiled and said, "Okay, Mom, I'll help Sissy cook one of my inventions!"

She leaned over and hugged her oldest son, then kissed him squarely on his lips. Standing up, she ruffled his hair. "Be good at school today," she said, more for Letty's benefit than Jacob's. After all, it was usually Blaise who got into trouble at school.

After the children were safely in the Johnsons' compound, Natazhia began the walk back home. Usually, she enjoyed the brief amount of peace and calm, however, this morning the quiet was almost unbearable. Would that be the last time that she held her two oldest children? Her mind drifted back to the words she'd read that morning. *Surrender. Control is but an illusion that separates you from Him.* Natazhia took a deep breath, looked up at the sky, and began a silent monologue. *I want to surrender, really, truly. I'm just not sure how to. If I let go and give up control, how do I know they will be safe? Okay, never mind, I get it; place my trust in You. I get that, and I do, I just—I feel like it's my responsibility to keep them safe. I'm trying to let go; seriously, I am. I don't know how, though. Please be patient and help me. Okay, so how's this? Lord, I'm asking for peace and trust in You, whatever the day ahead brings. Is that better? Now, You'll just have to remind me throughout the day that I've given control of this day to You. Ugh! And I still don't like leaving them alone.* Natazhia kicked a rock on the path as far ahead of her as she could. *But I'm going to trust You, God, to watch over them.* She pulled her old iPhone out of her jacket pocket. Ryker had long ago disconnected all services from the networks for their safety. However, Natazhia could still listen to music she had stored on the phone before the Liberation. Although she knew it was foolish and a potential risk to her safety, Natazhia put her earphones in and selected her classical playlist, hoping the music would keep her mind at bay.

Before she knew it, she was back at the opening in the blackberry bushes across from her gate. She tucked away her earphones and iPhone in her pocket. *Ryker would be angry if he knew I had been listening to music on the way home.* She understood, of course. Natazhia had been oblivious to everything for more than ten minutes. She completely lost herself in the beautiful sounds of the orchestras. Before emerging from behind the bushes, she took a few minutes to focus on her surroundings. She listened for any sounds that didn't belong, then peeked out and looked up and down the small dirt road. She quickly crossed the road with her hand on her pistol, unlocked the gate, and ducked in.

Safely inside their compound, Natazhia paused to tend to Hattie and the other goats. She walked over to the garden, pleased to see corn, lettuce, cabbage, and chard nearly ready for harvesting, with pumpkins and winter squash not too far behind. Not wanting to prolong the emotional goodbye, she filled her time by watering some of the garden. She knew Ryker was still busy packing up their goods and securing them to the three-wheeler. Her husband was meticulous when it came to packing, and she didn't have the patience to go inside and wait while he packed and re-packed such that he used every square inch efficiently. With the kids situated she was impatient to get on the road and get back as soon as possible. Nurturing her garden gave her something to do and also gave her a sense of peace. It was one of the few things that seemed to flourish in the world in which they lived. *Thank you,* she thought, looking up at the sky toward the sun with her eyes closed; *thank you for providing us with a beautiful garden.*

"Natazhia!"

Startled, she opened her eyes and spun around. She had not heard Ryker calling over the sound of the hose.

"Come on; the ATV is ready. Let's hit the road."

She walked over to the pipe that stood a few feet away from their water well, turned the faucet off, took one last look at the garden and her animals, and then walked back across the yard to the kitchen door. She found Blaise sitting at the table holding the radio.

"Don't worry, Mama," he said with a smile. "I'll be okay."

Natazhia walked over to the table, wrapped her arms around Blaise, and said, "I know; you are the strongest and bravest little boy I know." Inside, her heart was breaking. She lived in a cruel world that made it necessary for her twin boys to take turns hiding, and to leave her baby at home all by himself. She kissed him on the top of his head and said, "Remember, stay in the house. If someone comes, get to the attic. Only fire a weapon if you absolutely have to. We can do without almost everything in this house. I can't do without you, my little prince."

Blaise nodded. "I'll be good, Mama, I promise. I won't take one step outside."

Giving him one last squeeze, Natazhia added, "I love you, sweetheart. We'll be home as soon as we can be."

Ryker walked over and patted his son on the shoulders. "You're the man of the house for the day. Be a good boy and keep an eye out for any trouble. I'll see you soon."

Natazhia turned and walked outside; she couldn't bear to see the scared look on her son's face. He was trying so hard to be brave. She waited outside by the three-wheeler while Ryker locked the doors and did one last patrol around the house and the compound. Once he returned and climbed on the ATV, she climbed up on the back behind him, then pulled a rubber band from her jacket pocket and pulled her long hair into a ponytail. Ryker turned the key, and the old three-wheeler fired up. He drove it across the compound to the same gate she and the children had used earlier to go to the Johnsons' property.

"Get the gate!" Ryker yelled loud enough to be heard over the engine.

Natazhia jumped off of the ATV and pulled the key back out of her pocket, and opened the gate, wide this time so that Ryker could drive their three-wheeler through it. Once he'd cleared the gate, Natazhia closed and locked it, then grabbed the semi-automatic rifle off of the three-wheeler's gun rack and strapped it over her shoulder.

Both Ryker and Natazhia remained vigilant as they made their way down the narrow dirt road between the tall blackberry bushes that lined either side, concealing theirs and the Johnsons' compound. Natazhia and Ryker were confident that the community remained undiscovered by outsiders; however, unlike Natazhia, Ryker didn't take any chances. He instructed her to hold the rifle, ready to fire at any moment. It would be eight or so miles before they reached Old Highway 89A. Left unmaintained since the borders closed, it had deteriorated. If they remained undiscovered, they wouldn't see any traffic until they got there. There were people living in numerous compounds in Williams, Flagstaff, Cottonwood, Clarkdale, and Camp Verde who would head out to the trading post in Jerome. All would eventually travel along the old highway. It was too risky to keep the trading post open year-round, so word would get sent out once per quarter regarding the days it would open. Natazhia and Ryker preferred to get there on the last day or two. By then, the regular traders were more willing to discount their prices to avoid carrying inventory back to their camps. They were also more willing to pay top dollar for the hard-to-find and luxury items like Natazhia's soaps, candles, and quilts.

It took Ryker about thirty minutes to navigate the rough path and dirt road that spanned the distance between their compound and Old Highway 89A. Once they reached it, traffic was dense as they had expected. Natazhia kept a close watch for anyone who looked out of place. There were often new refugees along the route, but usually, they were traveling with familiar faces. They were more concerned that Liberation spies might join the ranks and attempt to gain valuable intelligence about their communities, supply chains, and weapons. Rebellion leaders hadn't reported any breaches near the old highways. Ryker had installed a CB Radio on the three-wheeler, which Natazhia monitored closely.

3

SURRENDER

Just over two hours after leaving the compound, Ryker and Natazhia arrived in Jerome. The narrow streets buzzed with activity from the base of the mountain to the top. Abandoned houses were perched precariously over the edge of the hill. Once known for beautiful pieces of art and jewelry, the storefronts now served as temporary storefronts for merchants carrying everything from fresh fruit and vegetables to hard-to-find medicines, parts for ATVs, and ammunition.

Ryker spotted an opening on the edge of the once beautiful park and pulled in by a tree, turning off the engine of the three-wheeler. Natazhia climbed off and slung the rifle back over her shoulder. Ryker chained the ATV to the tree. Then after handing Natazhia her pack, he threw his pack over his shoulder, untied the supply trunk, and hoisted it atop his shoulder. The couple began walking toward the crowded sidewalk.

"Is it just my imagination, or are there more people here this time?" Natazhia asked.

"No, it's not your imagination; there are definitely more people here," Ryker answered. "I think more and more refugees are finding places to build camp up here in the high desert."

"Perhaps it's time the Rebellion Leaders consider another trading post," Natazhia said. "I don't like not knowing all of these people; they could be Liberation soldiers for all we know, and—"

Ryker put his hand on her arm, and lowered his voice. "Natazhia, not now. This isn't the place to criticize the Rebellion Leaders; after all, they are the ones who've kept us safe for so long."

"Ryker, I didn't mean—" Natazhia whispered. "You know how I think out loud sometimes. I was just thinking."

Ryker said, "It's okay, I know. I just don't want someone to overhear and misunderstand. Let's talk about it when we get home. I'll try and find Grayson while we are here today and set up a meeting with him."

Grayson Doyle was a friend of theirs. Natazhia and Ryker sometimes served as volunteers at Rebellion Training Camps. Grayson had been the Chief of the volunteer staff at one of the camps. Ryker and Grayson had become good friends. They were very much alike, and Grayson, who was old enough to be Ryker's father, had become somewhat of a role model and confidant to Ryker. As close as Ryker was to Grayson, Natazhia found him highly intimidating. He was a long-time military man who had even served in the United States Army before the Libertarian Reform. Grayson was also brilliant. In Grayson's presence, Natazhia always felt as if she was somehow not enough.

"I hope I can still find the supplies we need," Natazhia said, changing the subject. "I only have five pounds of soap left in storage. We need the lye and oils to prepare for January's trading post."

Smiling, Ryker said, "I'm sure we will have no trouble finding your supplies. The merchants always seem to have a stash set aside for your soaps and quilts. If anyone ever figures out how to duplicate your handiwork, then we'll worry."

Surrender. Control is but an illusion that separates you from Him. The words from her morning reading flashed through Natazhia's mind once again, this time with anger. *All right, I get it. I don't need to control this situation. Fine, I'm trusting You, Jesus, to provide for us today!* Natazhia was frustrated with herself and the world around her. The Liberation had made it such that they had little to no control in their lives. She knew in heart, though, that she had to resist the temptation to control everything around her. Each time she thought of the reading that morning, she imagined a neon sign above her head that said, "Look! She failed again!" Natazhia suddenly realized that her earlier ranting to her husband was more about needing the trading post system to stay the same.

Sighing, she said, "Ryker, there is no need to talk to Grayson. I'm sure everything will be just fine."

"Are you sure?"

"Yes," Natazhia responded with more confidence, "I'll bet we find a better offering today because there are more refugees out here trading."

Natazhia liked to spend the first few hours walking through the different storefronts and tents scattered up and down the mountain before trading. Ryker preferred to catch up with old friends. He also refused to carry the trunk for the hours Natazhia spent window shopping. Unwilling to trust the minding of their goods with even the closest friends, Ryker remained at one of the tents at the bottom of the hill that served hot coffee and freshly baked bread with cinnamon. Meanwhile, Natazhia strolled from one merchant's shop to the next. Her favorite stop belonged to the clothier. As much as she admired the fine shirts and dresses that hung from his tent poles, she had no practical use for any of them. She preferred to sift through his box of fabric remnants. The remnants were of no value to him, so he was always willing to let her take as much as she wanted in exchange for a candle or two. It was a small price to pay for the high-quality fabrics, and Natazhia always found plenty to piece together enough squares to make a lovely quilt or two.

Sifting through the beautiful fabrics helped to soothe the anxiety she felt leaving the children that morning. It seemed to turn the trading post into a magical place where the world was all right, even if for only a day. When she arrived at the clothier's tent that day, she was surprised to see that someone else had replaced the usual trader.

Even so, after months of solitude on their compound with Letty Johnson as her only friend, Natazhia welcomed chatting animatedly with the short, plump stranger. Together they oohed and aahed over textures, colors, and prints. She found herself drawn to watching his hands as he waved them around while talking, adorned as they were with several large, flashy rings. Few refugees owned jewelry, and no one dared to wear the jewelry they owned. Ryker and Natazhia only held on to their wedding bands, and Natazhia kept a pair of delicate gold earrings in the shape of a cross that held tiny emeralds in the center. Wearing either of the items publicly put their lives in danger as any form of Christian worship was strictly forbidden. As marriage laws had changed through the years, wedding bands became more symbolic of religious rather than legal marriage. Even among the refugees, the idea of Christianity often caused division and arguments. Most felt as long as the communities weren't openly disobeying the Liberation's Rules, there was little cause for the Liberation to bother with them. After all, there was minimal land they occupied that offered The Liberation any natural resources. It made Natazhia uneasy that the clothier was comfortable flaunting so much jewelry on his chubby little hands.

Quickly stacking the remnants of fabric that she wanted to take with her, she pulled out a beautiful beeswax candle she had made from her pack, and asked, "Will this cover it?"

The clothier laughed obnoxiously. "Darling, I hardly think these fine fabrics are worthy of just one candle."

Usually, she would stand her ground, but there was something about this man that seemed out of place, so she said, "So, two, then? That's all I have in my pack."

"Very well, two it is, my dear," he said, taking the candles. "Have a fabulous day!"

Natazhia hastily stuffed the pile of fabric into her pack and awkwardly thanked the clothier, realizing she had never bothered to ask for his name. *Perhaps that was for the best; at least he doesn't know my name, either, I hope.* She rushed back down the hill to find Ryker.

The uneasiness she felt earlier when they arrived returned through her exchange with the clothier, and Natazhia was ready to make their trades and get back home to the children. As she rounded the corner, her heart started beating wildly when she noticed a crowd beginning to gather where Ryker had settled in for his coffee. She instinctively knew that something was wrong with the scene that was unfolding below her, and she kept running down the hill. Refugees all around had also noticed the commotion and started running down the mountain to investigate. Many merchants even abandoned their wares, curious about the unusual activity. She paused a moment to catch her breath and, for some reason, turned to look back at the clothier's tent. She could see the stranger simply standing there in front of his tent, arms folded with a smug grin pasted to his face. His demeanor sent a chill up her spine, and she turned away and ran even faster. *I've got to find Ryker; something is wrong,* she thought to herself as she reached the edge of the crowd.

Refugees were pushing and shoving one another, trying to get closer to the center of the crowd, each calling out the names of their loved ones.

"Ryker!" Natazhia yelled.

She couldn't hear any response from him above all of the chaos and shouting. The high-pitched squeal of a microphone too close to its source startled her. A "tap-tap" sound followed it through the speakers. Even more uneasy, she turned toward the sound coming from the center of the mob. Natazhia couldn't recall the last time she had been in the presence of such highly technical sound equipment. It had been something she took for granted as a child, seeing it in schools, churches, concerts, and political rallies. There was something about the equipment being here at their trading post that caused the hair on the back of her neck to stand up. She, along with the noisy crowd, suddenly fell hushed in silence, all turned toward where they'd heard the sound originate.

"Can someone pull one of those tables in for me to stand on?" The feminine voice behind the microphone sounded both calm and in command. "I'd like for everyone to be able to see me as best as possible."

I know that voice. Where have I heard it? Then it dawned on her. *The Rebellion Army's radio transmissions, I've listened to her on the radio when Ryker is monitoring communications. Who is that?* Someone must have brought a table over because the woman began to rise above the crowd. There were gasps as she stood up into view. The woman was breathtaking with thick flowing blonde hair, porcelain skin, and blue eyes that seemed to look right through you and into your heart. She stood silently and took her time to look out into the crowd. *It's Zyra Kim,* Natazhia realized. *Why is the Leader of the Rebellion Forces here at our trading post?* Whether or not she wanted the answers, she was about to find out.

"Friends," Zyra began, with all eyes on her, "our nation, our world has strayed far from that which our forefathers intended. They created a nation where every man and woman had certain inalienable rights. Before that, our creator placed us on this earth to love one another as He loved us."

Natazhia looked around as the crowd broke out in whispers. They were all as astounded as she felt at that moment. *Is Zyra talking about God the Father publicly? It can't be.*

"Yes, my friends, I am speaking of God. Our Father meant for all humanity to live on earth in peace and harmony. And yet, it is not so. The Reformed Liberation of America has turned its back on Him, and we all live with the consequences. And those consequences are grave."

Then Zyra fell silent. Natazhia was shaking. Zyra had a definiteness of purpose in everything from the words she spoke to the way she looked at the crowd, and even in the way she stood, with such power and compassion. Natazhia went up on her tiptoes, trying to see over the crowd. She felt a growing sense of urgency to reconnect with her husband and be close to him.

After a long pause, Zyra began to speak again, quieting her voice, indicating that everyone should listen closely. "In a few minutes, I am going to give you specific instructions to follow. Hear me when I tell you that the way you follow these instructions will determine our future. We have received reliable intelligence that suggests a chemical attack on our territory is imminent."

The crowd began to erupt in panic.

Zyra raised her hand and said firmly, "Ladies and gentlemen, if you will, remain calm. The rebellion forces are well prepared and have provided a contingency that may just spare your life. But for that to occur, you must remain calm and listen carefully."

The crowd quieted. Natazhia thought surely her husband was nearby, however the crowd was pressing around where she stood. The pounding sound of her heartbeat almost made it difficult to hear Zyra's next words.

"At the top of the mountain far below Holy Cross Church, an old mine shaft will take the future leaders of New World View to a life-sustaining bunker and training ground. There is only room for seventy-eight souls, and thirty-eight of them have already been recruited from the Southern Territory Trading Post and are safely inside. That means that there is only space for forty more."

Just as she finished her last sentence, the crowd began to run for the old church.

Within seconds, Ryker was at Natazhia's side.

She hugged him tightly, crying out with relief, "Oh God, I was so scared I wouldn't find you!"

"I'd have never let that happen," he said, grabbing her hand. "Come on, let's go."

Natazhia stood firmly in place. "Ryker, the children, we can't leave them."

He continued to pull her arm. "Love, we must go. I spoke to Grayson; we don't have time to get to them. He's going to radio help and get them in the bunker at home. If they can get in there, they will be safe."

Still hesitating, she said, "But what about Blaise, no one knows to find him, and he won't let anyone in."

Growing impatient, Ryker said insistently, "Natazhia, I trust Grayson Doyle; I told him about Blaise. He promised to send Serenity in the house to get him before they go to the bunker. There's no time! If there is any chance of us ever seeing the children again, we must get in the bunker. Now let's go!"

Still torn between trusting Grayson Doyle and the Rebellion soldiers to save her children or going after them herself, she followed her husband. As they ran up the hill, his final words began to sink in. *If there is any chance of us ever seeing the children again, we must get in the bunker.* The uphill run was a strain on her muscles, and Natazhia pushed past physical limitations to fight for her life and her husband's life.

As they reached the entrance to the old church, they found the crowd fighting, and some were even pointing their weapons at others. Ryker pulled Natazhia around the back of one of the three men who seemed to be doing everything possible to keep everyone out.

The men were yelling at the crowd pressing against them. "It's full; there's no room!"

As they slipped behind the men, Ryker said to his wife, "I'm betting they're pretty confident there is space for them. Come on."

Ryker and his wife just made it inside the church door and quickly headed down toward the basement of the church, assuming they'd find the entrance to the bunker down there. Huddling up against the wall with the others who had made it inside, Natazhia began counting heads. There were forty-six in the hall, pushing and screaming at each other.

"We were here first!" a woman shouted.

"It doesn't matter! You are too old to have children, and you don't belong here," another said angrily. "Get out!"

Natazhia leaned against the wall quietly. She desperately wanted to be in that bunker, yet something did not feel right about the way they had arrived there. *What makes me more deserving than anyone else?* Looking at Ryker, she said, "This isn't right!"

He nodded in agreement. "I know. Come on. I have a plan."

Ryker held Natazhia's hand and led her up the stairs to the entrance of the church. From the landing, he could see both the crowd outside and those below jockeying for position at the entrance to the bunker.

"Stop!" Ryker yelled.

No one seemed even to notice. Natazhia's husband placed two of his fingers in his mouth and let out a high-pitched, shrill whistle. For a moment, there was silence as everyone looked to see where the noise originated.

Ryker began to speak. "Men and Women, those who go below ground have an awesome responsibility for the future of this world. Is this how we select our future leaders?"

The crowd erupted in screaming and began pushing and fighting with one another.

Natazhia placed her hand on Ryker's shoulder. "You're a good man, Ryker. I'm proud of you, whatever happens."

Ryker's effort had not gone unnoticed. Natazhia looked over the crowd to see people shifting and making room for Zyra Kim to walk up to the landing where Natazhia and Ryker stood. Grayson Doyle and a man she didn't recognize set down the loudspeakers on the landing after carrying them up the mountain, following Zyra, who was still holding the microphone.

The Rebellion leader's voice was unbelievably compassionate and calm as she scolded the crowd. "Ladies and gentlemen, I believe a member of your community risked everything and stepped into a leadership role to address you. Yet, not one person gave him the respect he deserved. Why?"

There was complete silence. Zyra allowed the silence to go on for what seemed an eternity. "Really? Not one person in this uncivilized mob can answer that?"

Another long silence followed.

"Well, I think you know the answer, and you just don't want to speak it for all to hear." She paused and allowed another long, uncomfortable silence to give the crowd a moment to let her words sink in. "I'm going to give this man an opportunity to say what he wanted to say. But before I do, I have one question. Do you specifically recall who I invited to enter the bunker?"

A man in the front row spoke up. "Future New World Leaders," he said.

Nodding and smiling, Zyra said, "Yes, future New World Leaders. Ask yourself, are you behaving like a future New World Leader?" She turned and looked at Ryker. "Sir, what is your name?"

"Ryker Flynn, and this is my wife, Natazhia."

She smiled and shook her head. "Mr. Flynn, I didn't ask for your wife's name."

Stammering, Ryker said, "Uh, yeah. I'm sorry, ma'am."

Still smiling, she looked at him and said, "Well, Ryker, I'm going to hand this microphone to you and give you the floor. I hope whatever you planned to say is worthwhile."

"Yes, ma'am."

Zyra handed the microphone to Ryker, and he began. "When I was down at the entrance to the bunker with my wife, there were still people fighting for their position to get in, and the thought occurred to me that exactly this kind of behavior is what's wrong with our world today. We don't consider what is best for everyone, only for ourselves and those we love. Today many of you didn't even consider those you love. There are wives inside fighting for entry, unconcerned that their husbands are still outside. And, some men left wives at the bottom of the hill to be trampled by the crowd. Is this how we envision a New World? We have an awesome responsibility to create a world that works for everyone. To do so, we must ensure that we have people with the right motives. We need to know that we have a diverse community that offers all of the skills necessary to train the children of a New World. The community must offer medical care, leadership, builders, and scientists. Today is bittersweet. This world ends as we know it, and yet there is an opportunity to start over and build a world that works for everyone, where no one is left behind. Whether you go in that bunker today or not, you have an opportunity at this moment right now to do the right thing and make history."

Ryker handed the microphone back to Zyra.

"So, Ryker—" Zyra said, "tell me, how would you choose who goes inside the bunker?"

Ryker took a deep breath, and then leaned toward the microphone that she pointed to him. "Well, I would ask who had the necessary skills and credentials, then I would trust my intuition on which ones to pick."

Satisfied with his answer, Zyra spoke into the microphone again. "Very well, Ryker. Now, ladies and gentlemen, does anyone object to Mr. Ryker's statement?"

The crowd was once again silent.

Zyra smiled. "Good. Well, then that is how we will select our New World Leaders." She turned to those standing below at the bunker entrance and called to them. "You, yes, all of you! Come on back outside and stand in front of the church." Zyra watched as they filed out of the hallway below, walked up the stairs and past the three of them, then looked at Natazhia. "You, too."

Ryker and Natazhia started to walk hand in hand out of the church, but Zyra stopped them. "I didn't tell you to go, Ryker. I'm not finished with you, yet," she said, once again, smiling. "Mr. Ryker Flynn, since you have been the only man among many to demonstrate leadership under the most difficult of circumstances, I would like you to pick thirty-nine leaders to go in the bunker with you."

"Me?" Startled, Ryker said, "No, I can't be the one."

Zyra said, "Yes, Ryker, you are exactly the one."

He looked at the ground intently and was silent.

Natazhia knew he was holding back tears. She looked at him, and then at the cross that still rested atop the church, and prayed. *Lord, please grant Ryker the wisdom to choose only those You desire. Grant all of us peace no matter the outcome of this day. I release him, Serenity, Jacob, and Blaise unto You, for they were but mine only to watch over. Their future is Your will, as is mine. I understand now, and I am letting go. Amen.* Tears were now streaming down Natazhia's face. She knew that these next moments belonged only to God and His will. She was so very proud of her husband.

"Okay, I will choose. But if I choose, then I don't go," Ryker said.

"No, Mr. Flynn," Zyra replied, "it doesn't work that way. You don't get to choose, then stay behind, taking no responsibility for the choices you've made. You will choose your team, and then, you will lead them." She handed him the microphone.

Ryker took a deep breath. Then, turning to the crowd, he said, "Okay then, if you are a doctor or a nurse, please step forward."

Fifteen men and women stepped forward.

"Doctors, please raise your hands."

The field had narrowed itself to seven.

"Put your hand down if you are not a surgeon."

There were now four.

"Okay, then put your hand down if you have less than ten years' experience."

Only one dropped his hand. Ryker looked at the three men who stood before him for a few moments. "Okay, you and you, go down to the bunker."

Zyra walked back over to him and said, "Ryker, not to offend you or anything, but I did say that the chemical attack was imminent. Could you move a tad faster?"

Ryker smiled and let out a small laugh. "Yes, ma'am."

He continued his line of questions, asking for historians, teachers, plumbers, carpenters, scientists, attorneys, and judges, both men, and women, to help create new forms of trade and business. Natazhia was still standing with the crowd. Her husband had not chosen her, which didn't surprise Natazhia, given that she believed her skills were not as necessary as other ones in the New World. Within five minutes, Ryker had picked the thirty-nine.

Before giving the microphone back to Zyra, he said, "I have one more request, Madam Kim, if that is okay?"

"Go ahead, but make it quick."

"I want my wife, Natazhia, to go in my place," Ryker said. "She has skills in gardening, sewing, soap making, food preservation, and candle making. She's the one who prompted me to speak. It was she who recognized and showed me that the way we had secured entrance was wrong."

"Why then did you not choose her? It certainly sounds as though she belongs in the bunker."

"Yes, ma'am, I believe she does. I did not want to appear selfish and lose the respect of the chosen leaders by choosing my wife."

"Oh, so you wanted to look good, right?"

"Yes, ma'am, I guess so."

"So, you were more willing to let your wife die a horrible death rather than stand up and justify why you had picked her?"

Ryker looked over at Natazhia with sorrow in this new awareness of why he didn't choose her and said, "Yes, ma'am, I feel terrible." He looked at the floor below him, tears running down his cheeks.

"Ryker," Zyra said with compassion in her tone, "please understand this is not coming from a place of judgment; it's just feedback. So, you can do as you wish. I will honor your request, and Natazhia can take your place inside. And as for you, we need your kind of leadership at headquarters. So, you will be traveling with us."

Zyra motioned to Natazhia to join the men and women assembled at the bunker door. Then she turned to the group. "If you all choose to accept your position on this team, you must understand that the kind of feedback I shared with Ryker is the type of feedback you can expect to receive, and I expect you to give to one another going forward. I intend to create the strongest, most compassionate leaders to lead the New World. So, if you commit, please take a minute to say goodbye to your loved ones and return immediately."

Ryker and Natazhia held one another tightly, as the other chosen thirty-nine rushed back up to the landing toward their spouses, children, and close friends who pushed through the crowd to say their final goodbyes. The couple watched as a mother clung to her children, tears streaming down her face.

Natazhia turned to her husband, looking into his eyes, and said, "As much I wish I could hold our children and tell them how much I love them, I'm grateful they don't have to go through this."

Ryker nodded and very softly said, "Me too, me too."

Natazhia took a deep breath, placed both of her hands on Ryker's chest, and said, "I don't always say it; I know I should, and I'm sorry I haven't. I love you. You are an amazing man, father, and husband. I'm grateful for the time I've had with you."

Ryker grabbed her by the chin and made Natazhia look into his eyes. "Look," he said, "I will have none of that. This is not goodbye forever; it's just goodbye for now. We will survive, and goodness will prevail. Then together, we will find our children who will make it to the bunker and survive the attacks. Then, with the rest of these men and women, we will create a new world, one that works for everyone—"

Natazhia finished his sentence. "—with no one left behind."

They smiled at one another, tears falling from their eyes. "It was a beautiful speech, Ryker. I didn't know you had it in you."

Laughing, he said, "Me neither."

In the distance, they heard the sound of emergency sirens. "It's time to go," he said.

"I know," Natazhia said, catching a sob in her throat.

They kissed one last time and began moving in opposite directions, touching fingertips until they were too far apart. Once they could no longer stay connected physically, Natazhia placed two fingers on her lips, kissed them, and held them up, showing the sign for peace. Ryker responded by doing the same, and then they turned and ran in opposite directions.

Despite knowing she would not see her children that evening, Natazhia felt at peace for the first time all day. She believed her husband when he said they would find the children and be reunited. She was one of the chosen forty, and she knew what a tremendous responsibility that was. And she knew it was God's will. For the first time in twenty years, she could envision a world where she wouldn't have to hide her Christian beliefs and a world where women didn't suffer because the law required that their babies be taken violently from their wombs.

4

HOUSEKEEPING

Natazhia, one of the newly chosen forty, joined the others in making their way down the stairs to the hallway where she and Ryker had been jockeying for position. The group followed the stranger who had been with Grayson earlier, carrying the loudspeakers behind Zyra. As they moved away from the church's closed doors, the muffled sound of the chaotic crowd outside was more than Natazhia could bear. She could hear screaming, fighting, and gunfire amid the sound of the sirens, as the group erupted into a panic. Her heart pounding, the realization was sinking in that the world might finally be coming to an end. Guilt overwhelmed her, knowing that none of the people outside those doors would live to see another day. She ducked her head down, pulling the collar of her jacket up over her ears, hoping to block out the screams and cries.

The man leading them arrived at the end of the hallway and stopped. Full of anticipation, the group of forty came to a halt. Reaching for the chain that hung from his belt loop, the man pulled a large bundle of keys attached to the other end, and fumbled for a few seconds, then finding the right key, unlocked and opened the door to the bunker.

Further back in the group, Natazhia stared ahead at the man holding the door open for the chosen forty as they began to file by him. As she approached the open door, she could see he was about an inch shorter than her and looked close to her father's age if he were still alive. *Where is this man from? His skin is far too fair for him to have been a refugee in the free territory. Could there be other free territories? Is it possible we are not the only ones?* When it was her turn to enter, the man peered out from behind his glasses and, unsmiling, made eye contact with her. Embarrassed that he caught her staring at him, she blushed and quickly turned her gaze to the floor in front of her as she walked by him. While relieved to be inside, something about him left her feeling uneasy, as though she were somehow inferior and that he would be sure she never thought otherwise.

Beyond the doorway, Natazhia noticed the temperature drop significantly. It appeared they had entered an abandoned mine shaft. She had known there were mines in Jerome. The town had been established during the Gold Rush, long before Arizona had become a part of the former United States. She was astounded that the old church she loved to visit sat above one such mine shaft. *How is it none of the historical markers or history books revealed this mine shaft? Ryker and I thoroughly researched all of the known mines and even looked for those remaining unknown.*

The descent into the mine was steep. The walls were narrow, and the terrain was rough. Despite being located in the high desert, the tunnel was damp and dark. The only light was the dim glow of a flashlight held by one of the three men who had been holding off the crowd at the church entrance; he now led the way to the bunker. Natazhia found that maintaining her balance took almost all of her attention and focus. The others were also quiet, concentrating on every step. They remained silent except for the sound of heavy breathing and the random coughs that echoed throughout the cave from those who struggled to maintain their breath in the cool, thick, dampness. *We could be down here for months, years, maybe! If the air outside is contaminated, how will we have enough oxygen for all of us to survive?* Natazhia felt a chill run through her body as the man with the glasses made his way past her to get to the front of the group. He seemed to be reading her mind.

He turned to face them, and they all stopped walking in the dimly lit shaft. "Uh, hum!" The man cleared his throat and said, "Let's stop here for a moment. We are far enough away that we are safe from immediate exposure. I'm sure you are all concerned about your basic needs, and I can assure you, we will get to answering all of your questions when we arrive at camp. Allow me first to introduce myself. I am Allen Rice, one of the Lead Trainers. I will be working with you and supporting you in developing the leadership skills you must master for this team to create The New World View successfully. To the rest of the Lead Team, I am 'Professor.' If you so choose, you may also call me Professor; Allen is fine as well."

A woman standing behind Natazhia spoke up. "Um, Allen, or, uh, Professor?"

"Quickly, please. As I said, we are only safe from immediate exposure. I have word that smart bombs containing deadly chemicals are already airborne. We must get to the bunker."

Unaffected by his request for urgency, she went on. "Okay, well. I guess what I'm trying to say, I mean, is anyone else confused by all of this? I mean, what is it you want from us? I mean, I feel like there's all this secrecy and—"

Shut up already. Natazhia rolled her eyes and shook her head. For a moment, she was grateful for the darkness knowing no one else had seen her obvious impatience with the woman. *He just said he'd answer questions when we get where we are going, for crying out loud.*

"Aren't you listening?" Another woman spoke up. "He just said he'd answer all of the questions when we get there. And in case you missed it, he also said we were only going to be safe for a short time."

You go, girl! That's what I'm talking about. I'm going to like that lady!

"Well, excuse me, I don't know why you've got to get all in my stuff. I'm just speaking out for all of us who are confused," the first woman said.

"Look, I'm not in your stuff. And right now, you seem to be the only confused person. I think I speak for everyone else when I say the rest of us are clear that the chemicals could still kill us if we don't get moving. So, while I get that you are confused, I think all of us staying alive is way more important than helping you feel un-confused."

The confused woman continued. "Well, how do we know these people are telling us the truth? We don't even know there are chemicals or bombs—"

Just as she said the words, the mine shaft shook violently, and they heard the muffled sound of a loud explosion. Bits of dust and dirt sprinkled the group.

Allen called out in a loud booming voice. "The attacks have begun. We must take cover and get to the training camp. I don't know how long the shaft will hold if we continue to take hits of this magnitude." Allen unzipped his pack and quickly handed out chem lights to those nearest him who passed them around to the others.

The group began to run down the shaft, deeper and deeper under the earth's surface. They ran for twenty-five minutes.

We have to be at least a couple of miles in. The others who were running just ahead of Natazhia began to slow and then came to a stop when Allen stopped running.

"All right, team, we are about to leave the mine shaft and enter a natural cave that miners discovered a long time ago. There are some shallow areas, so please watch your heads." Allen stepped to the side and waited as each of them ducked to enter the cave.

The entrance to the cave was steep and rocky. Natazhia was confident the initial descent was well over thirty feet deep. She was thankful she'd opted for her sweater and jacket that morning. The temperature seemed to be dropping by the second. She could see her breath in the soft glow of the chem lights. As they reached the bottom of the cave floor, Natazhia shivered as she took in the darkness of the cave. Even with forty-one lights illuminated, she couldn't see the walls or ceiling of the cave.

"We have about another mile and a half before we get to the training site," Allen said as everyone stood in the center of the cave taking in its enormity. "Follow me; it's this way."

No one said a word for several minutes, leaving Natazhia time for her mind to wander. *I hope Serenity and the boys made it safely to the bunker.* As soon as she thought the words, a sense of peace washed over her entire being. *Thank you, Lord. I know in my heart that wherever they are, You love them, and they are at peace.* She wondered how soon she might hear from Ryker. *Certainly, Zyra Kim and her team will have some sort of communication with our camp. Ryker would be able to get word to me one way or the other if Grayson successfully moved the kids to the bunker. I need a distraction. The more I think, the crazier I make myself. One minute I'm good, the next I'm a basket case. Perhaps if I find someone to talk to, I can keep my mind off of my family.* She sped up and began walking in between different members of the group. *Maybe I'll find my friend who shut up "Dazed and Confused." I'll have to let my husband, and his intuition, have it for picking that one to come down here with us!*

It was challenging to see everyone's face, but she was sure the woman was tall. *She can't be that hard to find; she's probably the only one taller than me.* A few feet in front of her, she saw a curvaceous figure of a woman who was at least four inches taller than her. *That's gotta be her!* Natazhia lengthened her stride, and within seconds, she was walking side by side with the woman.

"Hi, my name is Natazhia Flynn. What's yours?" she asked, extending her hand in greeting.

"Hello," the woman said as she returned Natazhia's gesture with a weak, limp handshake. "My name is Racyne Brenner."

Natazhia tried to hide her surprise at the weakness of Racyne's handshake. She had expected this outspoken Amazon woman to return the gesture with a firm, strong grip; she had even braced herself for such a handshake.

"I appreciated how you handled yourself earlier," Natazhia said.

"It's no big deal," Racyne replied. "I just have no patience for the whole ditsy little blonde game."

"My husband usually has good instinct. I'm hoping that her behavior was just stress from this whole ordeal, and that's the last we see of the Barbie act."

“Well, you are way more optimistic than I am, Natazhia. I’m betting that one’s going to be trouble.”

“I hope you’re wrong,” Natazhia said hopefully. “What region did you come from today?”

“We hiked down from Cottonwood to re-supply at the trading post. We’ve only been camped there for a few days. We left Montana on foot about four months ago and have been working our way down south ever since.”

“We?”

“My fiancé and I,” she replied quietly. “We got engaged, and then I received word that I still have a brother living in the Tucson region.” She paused. “Well, maybe I still have a brother living there. I guess I may never know.”

“Oh, Racyne,” Natazhia said empathetically, “I’m so sorry. I don’t know what to say.”

“Doug, that’s my fiancé, is probably dead or at the very least suffering right now, and it’s all because I thought somehow that leaving the American Liberation and finding my brother would allow us the freedom to be parents. At least there, we might still be alive.”

“Racyne, you can’t blame yourself. Perhaps you would still be alive, but the Rebellion Armies will not go down without a fight. I’m sure they are retaliating with as much force if not more than the Liberation has directed toward the free territories. I don’t believe anyone above ground will survive this attack.”

“Do you have anyone out there, Natazhia?”

“Yes,” she said, hesitating before sharing more, “my husband, and our children.”

“Oh, Lord, I’m so sorry. So, you had two?”

Natazhia didn’t know how to answer her. *Does it matter now if anyone knows? I mean, they can’t possibly be in any more danger than they already are.* Finally, after a long silence as they walked together in the group, she replied, “Uh, yeah, something like that; you know, let’s change the subject. I don’t want to think about what’s going on out there.”

"I'm with you," Racyne said in agreement. "So, what do you think they have in store for us?"

"I can't even imagine," Natazhia said. "I mean, this is all so surreal. It's like they've been planning this forever. Ryker and I researched this entire region, and there was no indication that there was a mine or cave under that church."

"It is all rather mysterious. Who was that woman?"

"Do you mean Zyra Kim?"

"I guess," Racyne replied. "Remember, I've lived under the Libertarian Government my whole life. They only let us see what they want us to see."

"Oh, wow. I thought everyone knew who Zyra Kim is," Natazhia said. "She is the leader of an organization called the New World View."

"So, she's in charge of the Rebel Armies?"

"No, I mean, not exactly. The rebels cooperate with her, but Zyra believes in a more peaceful take-over of the Libertarian Government. The rebel armies offer protection for her organization in hopes that she will join them in creating a new government once they overthrow the Liberation Reform."

"If Zyra Kim has so much support, then why did she choose forty of us at random to come down here?"

"I don't know, Racyne. I mean, none of this makes any sense to me. And at the same time, when I'm in her presence, I feel like she cares about people. And it's like she can look at you and see right down into your soul. I can't help but trust her."

"You seem like a nice person, Natazhia, but trusting someone who lets a perfect stranger pick the only people who may survive the Apocalypse just seems like a terrible idea to me." Then remembering that the stranger was her new friend's husband, she added, "No offense, I don't mean anything against your husband, it's just— Well, she doesn't know him from the next guy."

Natazhia felt uneasy about her conversation with Racyne. *Oh, Ryker,* she thought, *I know you must have seen something I'm missing.*

“Well,” Natazhia said, defending her husband, “he’s a good man. What skills did he pick you for, Racyne?”

“Business. I’ve been CEO of several companies. If things weren’t so regulated, I’d be an entrepreneur. I’m fascinated by business and the way it works. I’d have given anything to be around in our parents’ days. I would have built some great enterprises. I sure hope your Zyra Kim is committed to rebuilding capitalism.”

It was the most excitement she had heard in the taller woman’s voice since they began their conversation. Natazhia was relieved to see that it wasn’t all doom and gloom with her. “I have to admit, I’m not at all versed in business.”

“Oh, sure you are. I mean, you were at the trading post. You’ve got to have some business sense not to get taken there. What do you trade?”

“I make quilts. They bring me the most in trade. And I also make soaps and candles. Besides that, I bring seeds, canned vegetables, and stuff like that from our garden.”

“See, you’ve got more business sense than you give yourself credit. You’ve got commodities everyone needs.”

Natazhia thought for a moment, then said, “I guess I never really thought of it that way before.”

“Well, it seems as though your husband was at least right in seeing that you had something to bring to the group. There aren’t many out there anymore who can create the way you do.”

The group ahead of them slowed down. There were others besides Racyne and Natazhia who had paired up and were engaged in conversation. They all quieted as the group came to a halt.

Allen cleared his throat as if to get everyone’s attention. “Uh, um. Well, we are here. Welcome to your home for the next five to six months, depending on how long before the war ends and it is safe to return to the surface.”

Five to six months? I never considered the idea of being down here for that long.

“In a moment, we will open the first set of doors, and you will enter a decontamination chamber. We don’t want to take any chances; therefore, you will enter the appropriate station for your gender. Men go to the left and women to the right. You will remove all of your clothing and place it in the bin provided. Afterward, you will step into the shower, where you will receive a high-pressure wash with antigens to combat any airborne chemical contamination that may have settled on your skin. After that, you will receive your uniform. Once you have put it on, you will exit through the archway, where you will receive a dry bath consisting of nothing more than extremely high-pressure air. The air ensures that anything removed in the cleaning process does not reattach itself to you or anyone else. Are there any questions so far?"

Natazhia raised her hand.

"Yes?"

"What happens to the clothes we are wearing?" she asked, afraid he may tell her she'd never see her mother's pants or her leather jacket again.

"If we determine they are uncontaminated, they will be cleaned and returned to your room."

"And if they are contaminated?"

"Well, then, miss, uh, um?"

"Flynn," she said, "Natazhia Flynn."

"Well then, Miss Flynn, if they are indeed contaminated, the specimens will be sent to our pathology lab for further testing and research. Once the lab has retrieved everything it needs for research and development of a vaccine and cure, they destroy the clothing."

"Thank you, Professor," Natazhia said, hoping there was no contamination.

"Very well," he went on, "if there are no further questions, I will continue. Once you have passed through the archway, you must remain in the staging area until everyone is complete. When the doors open, you have thirty seconds to enter the camp. Anyone who is not through the doors at that time will be left behind. Is everyone clear?"

Natazhia looked around, seeing that everyone was nodding their heads in understanding.

"Okay. Let's proceed with the decontamination process then, shall we?"

He pulled a small radio out of his pack and communicated to someone who must have been inside the camp. Seconds later, two very thick steel doors opened just wide enough for the chosen forty to file in one at a time. Natazhia and her new comrades filed into the room.

"Hurry! Hurry, ladies and gentlemen. We must limit our exposure to outside contaminants," Allen said, scolding them like children.

Natazhia followed Racyne. As she approached the changing station, Natazhia could feel a tug of anxiety around letting go of her leather jacket, comfortable boots, and the camouflaged pants that had belonged to her mother. *We were underground early enough not to have any contamination. They are just being cautious.* She tried to reassure herself. *I just need to cooperate; I'm sure they will return my clothes.*

At first, Natazhia welcomed the hot shower and high-pressure wash. The solar panels that heated their water at home provided lukewarm showers, and their well certainly didn't provide much pressure. However, after the initial rinse, the pressure increased, and her whole body was stinging as though her skin was being pierced by millions of needles. A person hidden behind a chemical suit and mask approached her. Natazhia assumed it was another woman, but she couldn't be sure. Standing slightly away from her, this person began to brush Natazhia's skin with a coarse, thick brush attached to the end of what appeared to be a broom handle. The antigen Allen had mentioned burned her already raw skin. Her heart began to race as Natazhia started to fully comprehend the genuine possibility she, her husband, and her children were not necessarily out of harm's way, even if they had all escaped the blast above ground.

Then she pictured her Bible and devotional resting in their hiding place. *I knew I should have put them in my pack, although I'm sure they will take everything, so if I'd brought them, they may well have confiscated them anyway.* Then she recalled Zyra standing on the table and speaking to the crowd. *She mentioned God! Perhaps this new world she wants to create will allow Bibles to be made and shared in print and digital collections.* The idea of a new world and her place in it intrigued Natazhia. She had stopped dreaming long ago. But as she considered the prospect of a world with Bibles and freedom, she also dared to imagine a world where Jacob and Blaise could go to school together and play outdoors with no fear. She thought of a world where her daughter wouldn't hide out in a compound to avoid harmful birth control shots and late-term abortions to prevent the unbalance of the male/female population. *Ryker and I could perhaps even fill our home with more children!* Natazhia's heart warmed with the idea that it may be possible to have another baby.

A muffled voice from behind the mask interrupted Natazhia's ponderings. "Move on."

Natazhia walked over to the clothing laid out for her. The uniform's material had a soft and supple leathery feel, yet it had more stretch than leather. The creamy color reminded her of the sweater she had worn earlier that day. Pulling the pants on, she was thankful for her healthy and slender physique. She thought of her new comrade, Racyne, and felt terrible for her. She seemed to carry a lot of extra weight around her torso. The creamy beige stretchy fabric would not be flattering. After pulling the long-sleeved tunic over her head, she reached for the wide, leather utility belt. At the moment her fingers touched the belt, her heart skipped a beat. *My holster! And my .380! They must be able to remove any contamination from those easily! I'll have to ask Allen about that as soon as I see him again.* Satisfied that the uniform they had given her fit properly and was comfortable, Natazhia walked through the archway where the blast of high-pressure air irritated her raw skin. She walked over to the corner of the room by the door that she hoped would soon take them to food and warm beds. Natazhia sat down on the floor, laid her head against the wall, and closed her eyes. She was exhausted. The others must have been as tired as she was because no one disturbed her.

After what seemed like only a few minutes, she woke, her heart racing as it had that morning when she thought she had overslept.

"Hey, Natazhia."

She looked up to see that it was Racyne who had said her name.

"Come on, Sleeping Beauty; it's time to go in and see this camp we've heard about all day! You don't want to get left behind, do you?"

"I don't know; right now, if it means I could sleep longer, I'm not so sure I'd mind."

"Well, I don't know about you, my friend, but I find it hard to sleep when I'm hungry. Since they've taken our packs, I don't think you'd last so long out here without food. Come on." Racyne reached her hand out to pull Natazhia up off the floor.

Extending her hand to accept Racyne's offer to help her up, Natazhia said, "No, I guess not."

"Don't forget, ladies and gentlemen, you will only have thirty seconds to get all forty of you through the doors. After that time, they will close, and anyone left outside will be left there with only himself to rely upon to survive."

Allen's voice was beginning to wear upon Natazhia. At times he genuinely seemed to care about their survival. Then there were moments when he seemed arrogant, as though believing he was more competent and more knowledgeable than any of them.

"Entry Available NOW!" He called out much louder than he had when he gave his instructions earlier.

Natazhia and Racyne were near the back of the line; the others were filing quickly ahead of them through the doors. Natazhia looked behind them to see the girl they had been referring to as "Dazed and Confused," with two others.

"Twenty-six, twenty-five, twenty-four," Allen called, counting down the seconds remaining until the doors closed.

Come on, people, MOVE! What is wrong with these people? Can't they hear him counting? She tried to push through those ahead of her. As much as she wanted to say something to get them moving faster, she was acutely aware of the fact that she would be living with these people for God only knows how long. She certainly didn't want to piss them off now by showing her bossy side.

"Sixteen, fifteen, fourteen, thirteen—"

I am not about to die because these people can't follow directions. Natazhia began to speed up, gently pushing those who were walking in front of her. They began to do the same thing, then a hefty man from behind her called out, pleading, "Please go a little faster; there are still a lot of us out here who don't want to be left behind."

"Nine, eight, seven—"

This is crazy; how are we supposed to get forty people through a door one at a time? This is impossible, especially when there are so many idiots in the front of the line who could care less who they leave behind. Natazhia was now being shoved from behind as she pushed those ahead of her. The numbers getting lower increased the urgency. There were only two or three people ahead of her. Her heart was racing.

Allen's voice droned on. "Three, two—"

Natazhia felt someone grab her by the shoulders, pushing her to the ground. Racyne almost trampled over her and the person in front of her as she charged past them through the door. Quickly picking herself up, Natazhia darted through the doors before the others could push past her.

"Securing Entry Immediately!" Allen yelled.

Relieved to be inside the room, Natazhia stepped to the left and leaned against the wall, then bent over to catch her breath and slow her racing heart. She was keenly aware that she had barely made it inside. She could hear yelling and banging on the outside of the almost closed doors. She knew that the "Dazed and Confused" girl and an overweight man had been behind her outside. After Natazhia got in, the heavy doors were moving way too fast for either to squeeze through without getting crushed. There was nothing she could do.

Natazhia straightened up and noticed the others were finding seats in the horseshoe shape of chairs. She scanned the room for Racyne. When she located her, Racyne returned her gaze and their eyes locked. Natazhia glared coldly at the woman whom she'd befriended only hours earlier. Turning away, Natazhia realized that two of the three empty seats would not be filled now. They belonged to the man and woman left outside to die. Her stomach in knots, Natazhia wished she would soon wake up from this awful dream. Still standing, she became aware of two people at the front of the room who she didn't recognize. One was a short woman with dark brown shoulder-length hair and eyes such a deep brown, they were almost black. The other was a tall, slender man with curly blond hair. Both of them had their eyes focused on Natazhia. She realized they were waiting for her to sit down, so she made a bee-line for the chair nearest her. Fortunately, Racyne was on the other side of the horseshoe.

As soon as Natazhia sat down, the dark-haired woman began to speak. She didn't take the time to introduce herself. Looking up at the man by her side, she said, "Is this the group of people who will hold the future of our world in our hands?"

"I'm afraid so."

"They don't even care enough about humanity to get out of their way to save one of their own."

"Yes, Tallia, that is exactly how I've experienced them these past few moments."

"Paul—"

"Yes, Tallia?"

"Go let the two of them in, please." She sighed.

"You got it." He rushed toward the double doors at the back of the room.

Natazhia looked over her shoulder to see Paul whisper something into a small radio. The doors began to open again, and in walked the man and woman who everyone thought had been left behind. The blonde-haired woman looked angry and walked with her head down and cocked slightly to the side. The man had tear stains down his dirty face but looked relieved and grateful that they had opened the doors.

"Well." Tallia began taking the time to make eye contact with each member of the group before finishing her sentence. "I'd like to hear what you have to say to these two human beings." Turning to the man and woman, she asked, "What are your names?"

The short, heavy man answered first. "Byron Shields, ma'am."

Tallia looked over at the woman who was still staring at the floor. The silence was almost deafening.

After what seemed like several minutes, the woman looked up, startled. "Oh, are you talking to me?"

"Yes," Tallia said, "I asked for your name."

"As if it matters to anyone here," she replied, "my name is Tristen, Tristen Marks."

"Tristen, it matters to me."

"If it matters so much to you, why would you play some damn game with us all by leaving us outside believing we'd die?" Tristen asked, her voice shaking.

"Because it matters that much, Tristen. You are the chosen ones. You are here because you are the leaders of the New World. The world is depending on you! Can they?"

"They can count on me, but I wouldn't be so sure they can count on the thirty-eight who left me outside to die."

"Yeah, we'll get to them in a minute," Tallia said. "I'm curious, though," she continued thoughtfully, "you say that you can be depended on to lead the New World. Do you even know what that means?"

"Well, I haven't thought about it. This is all pretty heavy, and it kinda just got thrown on our lap today."

"I know," Tallia said. "But if you took just a moment to consider it, what do you think it means?"

"I said I don't know. I mean, I guess I don't know what the right answer is."

Tallia smiled again. "Tristen, I'm not looking for a right or wrong answer. I'm looking for your response. I want to hear the answer that lies in your heart alone, not anyone else's."

"Well, okay, I guess it means that I'm going to lead people, make laws, protect others, and things like that."

The sarcasm and irritation in Tristen's voice as she responded to Tallia's question was clearly evident to Natazhia. Even though she felt immense dislike for Tristen, Natazhia hung on every word the women exchanged.

"Okay, Tristen," Tallia said. "I'd say it's highly likely that's the expectation, and more, as the New World emerges after the war."

For a moment, Tristen looked pretty happy with herself and her response. Still, her smile quickly faded and was replaced with anger as Tallia continued questioning her.

"So, then, Tristen, how do you expect to lead and protect others, or make laws for the benefit of others, when you don't care enough to take care of and protect yourself?"

"Hey, I was taking care of me!" Tristen fired back angrily. "Your other so-called leaders just threw me under the bus!"

"That may be true. And don't worry, I'll get to them." Tallia paused and looked around the room. "You all do know that you're not off the hook, right?"

Natazhia straightened up in her chair a bit. *That woman has been a pain in the "you know what" since we started. It's no wonder no one wanted to help her.*

Tallia's eyes rested on Natazhia as if she knew exactly what she was thinking. Natazhia silently released a sigh of relief when Tallia looked back over at Tristen and continued with her line of questioning. "Tristen, you are still responsible for yourself. Why on earth would you put yourself in the position where you didn't make it in the room, believing that you would die outside those doors?"

"Well, I guess if you're going to say I did it to myself, then I guess it's because I didn't see any reason to be further up in line with all these people. They've not exactly been friendly to me, especially her," she said, pointing to Racyne.

"So, are you saying that because you believed these people in this room didn't like you, that you intentionally stayed behind to die?"

"No, now you're putting words in my mouth. I'm saying that I was at the end of the line with Byron because I knew they didn't want me around them."

"Okay, so you know what they think about you, which is why you were at the end of the line, right?"

"Right. Wait, no, I mean, I don't know what they think." She made a sweeping motion around the room with her arm. "I know what she thinks," Tristen said as she pointed to Racyne. "And I'm pretty sure she thinks the same," she continued, this time pointing directly at Natazhia. "But no, I guess I don't know what all of them think. It still doesn't change the fact that if they cared at all about everyone behind them, they might have picked up the pace."

"If I understand you correctly then, Tristen, you are saying that you have no responsibility whatsoever in the events that led to you not getting in this room?"

"Right. I didn't cause the line to move too slow or the fight between those two." She nodded her head toward Racyne and Natazhia. "And, I certainly wasn't going to push people around and yell at them just to get in the doors; that would be rude."

"Okay," Tallia said, nodding, "I think I understand. You and Byron are victims because of where you were in the line, and you would rather die than be perceived as being rude?"

"Well," Tristen said as she looked down with her head cocked slightly to the right and smiled, "it sounds pretty silly when you put it that way."

Natazhia noticed that the heavier man who had been left outside the doors had tears streaming down his face once again.

Tallia must have seen too because she looked over and said, "Byron? That's your name, right?"

"Yes, ma'am, Byron Shields."

"Byron," Tallia said, grinning, "I'm sure I'm quite a bit younger than you; please don't age me by calling me, ma'am."

The rest of the group seemed to appreciate that Tallia was joking around, lightening the mood a bit, and they showed their appreciation by laughing along with her.

"So, what's all of the emotion about, Byron?"

Tears rolled down his cheeks even faster, and his voice was choked between the sobs. "Well— Oh, man— Uh, I don't even know what to say."

"Byron, I'd like to hear it from your heart. What's causing all of the emotion?"

"Aahhh." He groaned. "I, uh hem, well, while I was listening to, um, Tristen, I guess I, uh, oh man, this is hard."

"Byron," Tallia said, interrupting him, "it's only hard if you make it hard."

He paused and looked up as though he was thinking about what she had just said before he continued. "I don't think I'm making it hard; it's just that I, I, um, I realized that I let everyone else go ahead and didn't even expect that I would get in. And, I didn't feel like it mattered. I mean that I mattered. I guess when you're overweight like I am, you don't feel like you have anything to contribute. So, I mean, yeah, some guy picked me and all, but when you are heavy and all like me, you can't keep up with younger, thinner people or contribute near as much."

"So, Byron," Tallia said with her voice filled with compassion, "thank you." She bowed her head toward him. "Thank you for being the teacher of the moment and for sharing your heart. I'd like to make a request, and this is for all of you, not just Byron." She looked around the room before continuing. "When sharing, please speak from 'I.' What I mean by that is, Byron, did you notice that when you talked about being overweight and your feelings, you used the word 'you,' which detaches you from the emotion. Besides, there's no way you could know how I feel about my weight and what that means to me." She looked around the room again. "Does that make sense to everyone?"

There were nods around the room.

"Byron, thank you once again for being the teacher at the moment. Are you open to sharing very quickly from the place of 'I'?"

"Sure, I'm willing to give it a try; I didn't feel like I mattered." He emphasized the word "I" each time he said it as he continued. "Since I'm overweight, I don't feel like I have anything to contribute and I can't keep up or contribute the way young, thin people can."

Smiling, Tallia said, "Thank you! That was much better!" She turned away from Byron and asked the group, "How did that feel and sound different the second time Byron shared replacing 'you' with 'I'?"

Racyne answered. "He sounded stronger, more empowered."

Everyone was nodding.

"Yes, I agree," Tallia said, then asked, "anyone else?"

Natazhia answered. "It seemed like he was taking responsibility, while before, he sounded like a victim."

"Yes!" Tallia exclaimed. "Do you see how powerful the words you chose can be?"

They were all nodding. There was a noticeable shift in the energy of the room. The earlier tension and fear had been replaced with wonder and, perhaps even amid war, safety.

However, Tallia seemed opposed to the team's comfort because she quickly shifted the conversation once again after looking around the room. "Byron and Tristen, welcome. We are glad you are here. Thank you for your honesty and willingness to explore your hearts. I hope this will be the start of you both honoring and taking care of yourselves. This new world needs you, and for you to be your best, you must first take care of your physical, spiritual, and mental needs. As for the rest of you, we have not yet finished this conversation."

Once again, there was silence in the room. Most of the forty were looking at either their hands or feet. The air felt stifling as though one could cut it with a knife. Some, like Natazhia, were quietly looking around the room, analyzing each other. Being seated in the horseshoe configuration of chairs, it was the first time since they'd left the trading post for them to have a good look at one another. The silence was uncomfortable, yet no one was willing to break it.

Tallia looked over toward the doors where the man she had referred to as Paul still stood. "Paul, would you mind stepping in here for a few moments. I'm not sure I will keep my opinions at bay with this bunch."

"Sure, Tallia," he replied almost too eagerly. In many ways, he reminded Natazhia a bit of a puppy dog, cute, eager to please, with way too much energy.

"Ladies and gentleman, I'd like to introduce to you my excellent friend and colleague of more than ten years. This man is a father, husband, friend, confidant, and one of the most honorable, ethical, bold leaders I know. You will have an opportunity to know his heart, his strength, and his courage over the next several months while we prepare you to lead the New World: Mr. Paul Cullin."

"Thank you, Tallia," Paul said as he walked toward the center of the horseshoe. "Well, I suppose Tallia would like for me to find out why the rest of you left two members of your team behind to die."

"Well, yeah, that would be a great place to start!" Tallia retorted sarcastically from the seat she had taken just outside of the horseshoe after introducing Paul.

Paul grinned at Tallia. "You're not going to keep your opinions to yourself even if I address this issue, are you?"

"Probably not."

"Okay, well, just try and be nice, will ya?"

"I'm not going to make any promises. Go ahead; the floor is yours."

Natazhia found it hard to believe the two weren't more than friends. They bantered back and forth in an almost flirtatious way, reminding her of how she and Ryker, years before, had chided one another when they began dating. The thought brought a sharp pang of anxiety to her heart as she remembered she still had no idea if her husband and children were dead or alive.

"Well, uh hmm," he began by clearing his throat, "I think I'd like to hear from the first person who entered the room. Where are you?"

The room fell silent. No one spoke. Everyone looked curious to see who had been first in the room and what was in store for that person.

Finally, Allen Rice, who had a clear vantage point, spoke. "Um, well, er, I, uh, I think it was that man there," he said, pointing to an attractive young man with the bluest eyes Natazhia had ever seen belonging to someone with such a dark complexion and brown hair. She found herself wondering if they were his natural color.

"Thank you, Professor." Paul looked over toward the man Allen had pointed to and asked, "Sir, was it you who came in first?"

"Yeah, I guess it was."

"You guess?"

"No, I mean, yes, it was me."

"Okay, so before I ask you about your experience, can you share with us your name?"

"Sure, I'm Loren Grey; I'm from the White Mountain Region."

"Okay, Loren, so you were the first one in the doors. What was that like?"

"Well, I don't know that it was really like anything. I mean, I didn't see any reason we wouldn't make it in the doors, so I just walked in and sat down to rest. I began traveling overnight. We are quite a way from the trading post in the White Mountains, and I'm tired."

"So, not once were you aware that not everyone would make it?"

"No, man, I mean, not really. I guess I was aware when I heard the fighting between the two women at the doorway."

"Okay, fair enough." Paul stood there with one arm folded beneath his right elbow with his chin placed in his right hand. He stroked his beard with his fingers as if he were in deep contemplation. "I'm just wondering, how did you react when you heard the fighting?"

"Well, it wasn't really fighting. I just heard a noise as one woman pushed the other out of her way and knocked her down. It happened so fast there wasn't time to react."

"So, you were oblivious to the countdown and how many were left outside until you heard the commotion. Is that what I'm to understand?"

"Yeah, as I said, I just sat down in my chair and honestly almost fell asleep."

"You don't need to answer me, Loren; I'd just like for you to consider how often in life you put your comfort and needs before others around you. And how often you are oblivious to what's going on in the space you occupy."

Paul didn't give Loren a chance to reply. Instead, he asked, looking around the room, "Who are the women he was talking about?" To clarify, after a brief pause, he added, "the ones who fought to get in."

Natazhia glared at Racyne again and raised her hand. Racyne slowly followed her lead and also raised her hand.

Paul looked at Natazhia first. "Explain to us what the fighting was all about, would you?" Then he added as an afterthought, "But first, tell us your name and where you are from, actually, so I don't have to keep asking. I would appreciate it if, when you do share, that you first share your name and homestead and also stand up so we can all see and hear you."

Natazhia stood up nervously. Her cheeks felt hot and flushed, and she was uncomfortable standing and speaking in front of the room of people. *I just know I'm going to say the wrong thing.* "Well, ah, I'm Natazhia Flynn. We homestead in the Sedona/Oak Creek Canyon region. I wouldn't say it was exactly a fight. Racyne grabbed me from behind and pushed me out of the way. I mean, I made it in the room, but barely."

"Racyne, you said?" Paul asked to clarify, and Natazhia nodded. "Racyne, will you stand up also?" Natazhia started to sit down, but Paul stopped her. "No, Natazhia, don't sit down yet. I haven't finished with you." He continued once Racyne stood up. "Introduce yourself, Racyne, and then share with us what was going on for you at that moment."

Racyne sounded extremely defensive as she began. "I'm Racyne Brenner, and my fiancé, Doug, and I are, or I guess for him, *were* refugees from the Montana region of the Reformed Liberation of America."

Natazhia thought she could see tears well up in Racyne's eyes and even heard some sadness in her voice when she talked about her fiancé, but if it was there, it only lasted a second.

"Everyone ahead of us was moving so slow. I mean, you could hear Professor counting down, and there were only seconds left to get in the room. I guess I just reacted out of survival. She wasn't moving any faster, so I just pushed her out of the way so I wouldn't die."

"Racyne? I'm curious. Was it possible that you could have pushed both of you into the room, thus saving you both?"

"I never thought of that; I just figured it was her or me that was getting into the room, and I didn't want it to be her."

"So, it had to be 'either or' rather than 'both'?"

"Yeah, I never thought of it that way, but I guess so."

Paul addressed the whole group. "Let's acknowledge Racyne for being the teacher in the moment."

Seriously? Natazhia thought to herself. *She tries to kill me, and we are going to acknowledge her?*

"How often do you all make decisions from a place of telling yourself, 'I can either do A—or I can do B'?"

Almost every hand in the room went up. Natazhia felt awkward still standing in front of her seat and slowly raised her hand too. Racyne had already sat down.

Paul went on. "What if you were to choose to do both? Racyne, I'm going to suggest that there was a way you could have saved yourself and Natazhia and that this scenario did not have to be one that was either you or her. Does that make sense, everyone?"

Once again, everyone in the room was nodding.

Natazhia agreed with Paul but felt self-conscious standing while everyone was sitting. She slowly started to sit back down, hoping the conversation was over, but his eyes caught hers as she did so, and he said, "Natazhia, I'd have been pretty ticked off if Racyne pushed me out of the way. Why don't you share with us what you were feeling and thinking before and after she pushed you?"

Natazhia straightened up as she began to speak. "Well, I guess before she pushed me, I could hear Professor counting down, and I knew we wouldn't all make it in unless everyone ahead of us moved faster. As Byron said, I thought about yelling at them to move faster or even nudging them forward, but I didn't want to be rude. And then, out of nowhere, she just grabbed me by my shoulders and pushed me aside, knocking me down. I got up as quickly as I could cause I heard Professor call out 'two,' and I didn't think about anything except getting in the doors, so I just got up before anyone had time to react and step over me and I got in. After that, I thought a lot of things. I wanted to kill her. I mean, she had almost killed me by pushing me out of the way. I thought we had become friends throughout the day walking into the mine shaft. I had her back and expected the same. So, I guess I also felt betrayed. Once I got in and saw the doors closing with Byron and um, ah, Tristen still outside, I felt sick. I was angry. I mean, why couldn't everyone else have moved faster? They all heard the same instructions I heard, and they could hear the countdown. Why couldn't they all move with more urgency?"

Some of the forty began speaking over each other.

"Natazhia, we didn't know how many were behind—"

"—All of us could only go as fast as the person in front."

"I couldn't hear the countdown from in here—"

Natazhia stood still; she was growing angrier by the second, listening to all of the excuses from those who had made it safely inside the room.

"Natazhia, what do you think when you hear their responses?" Paul asked.

"Honestly?" she said, not waiting for Paul to answer before she continued, "I think it's a bunch of crap. Everyone heard the same instructions from Professor. They only cared about themselves."

"Don't hold back, Natazhia," he said, and as several of the others laughed, Paul questioned her further. "What if what they are saying was truly their experience, Natazhia?"

"I'm not sure what you mean, Paul."

"Well, what if they couldn't hear the countdown from where they were? What if they couldn't see what you could see from where you were? If you had called out to them to move faster or perhaps even pushed them a little to get them moving faster, could you have created the urgency required to get Byron and Tristen in the room too?"

"I suppose so, but why are you only calling me to the carpet for what I didn't do? I mean, if Racyne hadn't wasted time pushing me to the ground and causing that commotion, they may have gotten in too."

"Natazhia, I don't mean to call attention to you, but from all of your shares so far, you had thought of solutions. No one else shared that they had even considered calling out or pushing or even aware that you all wouldn't make it in. You did, and you didn't act on those thoughts. One of my mentors once suggested that the most insidious takers in the world are those who have the answers but don't act on them. I'm not suggesting that's what you are, but I would ask you to consider why you didn't act on your instinct."

Paul's words cut like a knife. Natazhia tried to hide her hurt and tears with anger instead. "If I had yelled at everyone to move faster or pushed anyone, you'd all be complaining about what a jerk I was."

"Maybe," Paul said, "but we'd all be alive."

Natazhia responded sarcastically. "We all are alive. This whole thing has been some sick game you all are playing for who knows what reason." She sat down, making it clear to Paul and everyone else that she was no longer participating in the conversation.

Tallia stood back up, walked over to the horseshoe's center, and stood next to Paul. "Can I interrupt, Paul?"

"By all means," he said, smiling, and motioned for her to take the floor.

"Natazhia, you are correct; no one died." Tallia paused for emphasis. "Today." Turning away from Natazhia, she began speaking to the entire room. "But the reality is our world is at war. What we once knew of the land above ground is forever changed, and we have no idea what the future holds. The next time, it could very well be life or death. You all are among the only humans who even have a chance at creating a new future, a new society, a new world! We will continue to provide opportunities for you to learn more about yourselves and your belief systems. Some of those belief systems serve you and will serve the people of this planet, and some of those belief systems don't serve you and could bring harm to the people of this planet."

She looked over at Paul and asked, "Do you think these guys are ready for a meal?"

Everyone began to nod eagerly.

"Um, yeah, by the looks of them all, I'd say so."

"Well then, let's shift and move. For all of those who shared, thank you once again for being the teachers in the room. I hope all of you will share. Before we leave to eat our dinner, I'd like to introduce the rest of my team and go over some basic rules of engagement. You will have an opportunity to either stand in agreement to the rules of engagement or disagree, in which case you may choose to leave."

Racyne spoke up with frustration in her voice. "That's not much of a choice; I mean, if we leave, we die."

"Not necessarily, Racyne," Tallia said. "We will provide you directions back out of the caves that lead to an area that we believe was not affected in today's bombings. Of course, we don't know what you will find, how long-lasting the chemicals are, or if survival is possible. This type of chemical attack has never occurred in our history on such a large scale. Of course, it is a safer and more controlled environment here inside the shelter, but we believe there will be other survivors from today's attack. You are free to leave the safety of the shelter and see what other opportunities are out there."

Racyne didn't respond. After a few moments of silence and no further interruptions, Tallia began writing on an electronic screen that hung behind her at the center of the horseshoe with a thick silver stylus. Before doing so, she raised her wrist to her mouth and said, "Black." She had a broad silver band with what appeared to be several stones of some kind on her wrist. Natazhia was intrigued as she watched the stone-shaped things light up and blink through several colors before they seemed to be onyxes. The words she wrote on the electronic screen were the same color as the stones on the bracelet.

1. Be on time.

   "I want you all to be clear about what I mean when I say 'be on time.' Each time we break, whether for a meal, free time, or in the evening, you will receive instructions about when and where to report. Being on time means everyone will be at the place where you are supposed to be on time. And that means all of you. If it is in this room, on time means you are in your seats, with your journals and stylus, which will be provided to you after the meal break, along with a hydration pack. You are to have nothing else at your seat unless instructed otherwise. Are there any questions?"

After a long silence, Tallia said, "Good," then turned her back to the group and began writing on the board again.

2. You are responsible for your safety.

   "So, here's the deal on safety. We are training for battle. Many of the exercises will be strenuous, and some will be challenging. You are responsible for your safety. If you must choose out of a training exercise to remain safe, your responsibility is to do so. Any questions on safety?"

3. Confidentiality.

   "Confidentiality is perhaps the most important rule of all. Everything said in this room is to remain confidential, and only if you have express permission from the individual who shared the information would you repeat it outside of the room. We will be sharing military intelligence with you that must remain confidential for the sake of the world mission. And you will be sharing personal information with one another so that you can dig deeper into your subconscious and eliminate all limiting belief systems. This room will be a safe place for you to do so. The media infected the world above with propaganda that has altered your subconscious. The propaganda has limited you and your capabilities. We will dig deep. Confidentiality will also extend to your living quarters, squads, and training partners, which will all be assigned later. What I mean by that is anything shared between partners remains confidential and not shared with

> others. The same goes for anything shared in your living quarters and squads. The only exception is in the case of safety. If you are aware that someone will harm themselves or someone else, we expect you to break confidentiality by bringing it to the leadership team's attention. Understand?"

Tristen asked, "Who's the leadership team?"

"I'm so glad you asked that, Tristen. I've been waiting to introduce everyone to you. Before I do, are there any questions regarding the rules of engagement?"

No one spoke; they were thinking about dinner.

"Okay, you all, come on up here with me." Tallia motioned to the others who were seated behind the horseshoe. "You've all met my right hand, Paul Cullin. He is the Commander of Weapons and Physical Training and will facilitate the vast majority of your weapons training and strength and fitness training. He will also co-facilitate all of your psychological and leadership training with me. If Paul is my right hand, Grayson Doyle is my left. I'm afraid he is not yet back from his current mission, but he is the Commander of Logistics, and I am sure you will meet him by morning."

Natazhia's heart skipped a beat. *Ryker is with Grayson! Will he be here, too? If not, at least when Grayson returns, I might hear news of my husband and Serenity, Jacob, and Blaise.*

Tallia must have noticed the smile that crossed Natazhia's face because she asked, "Natazhia, do you know Commander Doyle?

"He and my husband are friends. I believe my husband may be part of the mission he is on now."

"Your husband must be Ryker Flynn. I didn't connect the last name earlier. He's a good man; you are a very blessed woman," Tallia said with what appeared to be a knowing smile.

I hope so, Natazhia thought. *Does Tallia know that they went after my children? I wonder if she knows if they are all okay? Is that why she's smiling?*

Tallia continued her introductions, giving Natazhia some reassurance as she did so. "The last word I received is that Grayson is on schedule to return later tonight and will be with us during our first session tomorrow morning. My friend, Allen Rice, is responsible for bringing you all here safely. He will be one of the lead trainers along with three others we selected after watching you throughout the day and reviewing backgrounds. Would the following individuals please join us?" Tallia called out the names one at a time. "Holly Love, Jerome Neil, and Loren Grey."

Really? Loren Grey? He's been utterly oblivious to what was going on around him!

The three stood up and joined Tallia, Paul, and Allen at the center of the horseshoe.

"Professor, Holly, Jerome, and Loren will be your Lead Trainers. Professor shall be their Chief of Staff and liaison between the Lead Trainers and my team. In a few days, we will select five of you to be Squad Leaders, and then we will divide you all into five squads. I believe we have done enough for one day. Wouldn't you all agree?"

Everyone, including the commanders, lead trainers, and those left without specific roles, nodded emphatically.

"Very well then, Allen, would you please take everyone down to Arturo's Kitchen and give them instructions for the rest of the evening and tomorrow morning?"

"My pleasure, Tallia!" Allen turned to the group. "Okay, everyone, follow me again."

5

A NEW NORMAL

From the podium, Tallia raised her wrist in the direction of the double doors, and Natazhia could see the stones on Tallia's bracelet quickly shift from black to bright green. Immediately, the doors swung wide open. Tallia appeared to be communicating her commands without saying a word, and the bracelet executed her command as it changed colors. Natazhia had never seen anything like it, and she wondered if it was the same technology once trialed on unsuspecting humans many years ago that paired their thoughts with electronic devices. The idea made her uneasy.

With some bewilderment, the group walked through the doors into the narrow hallway, following Allen when he turned to the right. Earlier, when they arrived from the other direction, it appeared that the hallway ended just beyond the entrance to the room. Natazhia hadn't noticed the doors to the right, which were now wide open. As they passed through the entryway, this section of the hallway was vast and brightly lit. It seemed out of place, in comparison to the small tunnels and halls they had traveled throughout the day. Art adorned the walls, illustrating all eras of the country's history including paintings of former presidents, aircraft, and depictions of every war and conflict. As they passed numerous doorways, Natazhia was increasingly curious as to what was hiding behind each one. It was still hard to believe the compound rested below the church, a place she and Ryker thought they knew inside and out. As they neared the end of the hallway, there was another set of doors she couldn't even see before they suddenly parted, seeming to slide backward and then slide to each side behind the walls. As the doors opened, a fragrant smell of garlic and freshly baked bread hit everyone at once, delighting their senses.

Natazhia hadn't realized how hungry she was until her stomach grumbled. She wondered what time it was. She hadn't eaten anything since she and Ryker had left their compound earlier that morning. The others must have been hungry, too. They all rushed toward the back corner of the room, where already-served-up plates filled with warm bread, fresh salads, and pasta with meatballs in rich tomato sauce topped with melted cheese waited for each of them. They sat down at the tables quickly and in silence. After a long day full of unexpected events with little to eat, they were much too focused on the food in front of them to talk.

Natazhia was deep in thought when Tristen roughly nudged her and asked, "Hey, you gonna finish that?"

Startled, she protectively wrapped her arm around her plate. "Of course, I just happen to take time to enjoy my food as it goes down."

Laughing loudly, Tristen said, "Well, it helps if you put it in your mouth first."

Natazhia looked down at her plate and realized she hadn't even touched her food. She picked up her plate and walked over to an empty table. She had so many thoughts racing through her mind. She was worried about Serenity and the boys, and she desperately hoped for some sort of message from Ryker. *Certainly, he knows something by now.* After being lost in her thoughts, Natazhia finally focused on her dinner plate, wondering where all of the food had come from. The meatballs tasted like ground beef, but cows had been impossible to raise in any state without water to grow grass for hay. It was all she could do to keep her goats alive, and yet here, in the bunker, there was enough food for all forty of them, and who knew how many others were underground with them. *How is this even possible?* She continued to savor the food on her plate even though she didn't understand where it came from.

As Natazhia finished up the last few bites, Tristen and Racyne plopped themselves down on the bench on either side of her.

"So, what's up, lady?" asked Racyne. "Did I chew with my mouth open and offend you, or are you always a loner?"

"Nah," Tristen answered for Natazhia, "she didn't appreciate me drooling over her plate."

Natazhia looked back and forth between the women, unsure why they felt the need to invade her space, then suddenly burst out laughing. "I'm sorry, no, it's not anything either of you did or said. I just needed some space to process everything we've been through today. I'm worried about my kids."

Tristen's eyes widened. "Oh shit, you have kids? Well, where are they? Why the hell would you leave your kids alone? How old are they?"

Racyne must've felt the need to protect Natazhia despite their earlier disagreement in front of the group. "Hey, back off, Tristen," she hissed. "You don't know anything about her or her family, and she sure as hell doesn't need your opinions about parenting."

"It's okay, Racyne, I can manage," said Natazhia, nodding at her friend. "Tristen, yes, I have children. My daughter is fourteen, and my sons are, uh—my son is six. Today, they were at our neighbor's house following their normal routine while Ryker and I left for supplies. Ryker and Commander Doyle radioed for help earlier today. So yes, my thoughts are a little bit preoccupied with wondering if they're safe."

Tristen stammered, embarrassed by her earlier accusing tone. "I'm sorry, I didn't mean, I mean, I never had kids and don't even know anyone with kids. I can't imagine what today must be like for you. I mean, what if you never hear anything, or like, you never know, like, how could you live with yourself? And—"

"Okay, Tristen, enough," said Racyne.

Tristen shrugged sheepishly. "Oh man, I'm doing it again. I'm sorry, I'll just shut up now. I can be so awkward."

Natazhia smiled. "It's okay; I know it's not easy to understand why someone would bring kids into a world like ours. I guess I'm a dreamer and have hope. Hope—that if we raise future generations with character and faith, that maybe, just maybe, all that's wrong with our world now, they can somehow turn it around and make it right. I have to believe that is possible. Otherwise, how could I look at their sweet faces each morning? They are my hope. We may not see freedom again in our lifetime, but I have to believe they might make it possible for their children."

Satisfied, Tristen responded. "That's cool, you got more faith in humanity than me, but that's cool."

"I wonder what's next," Racyne said somewhat absentmindedly and not really directed at anyone in particular as she looked toward the doors.

"Sleep! I hope," exclaimed Tristen. "Didn't they say we'd see our dorms?"

The wide doors slid open as if on cue, and Grayson, Zyra, and Ryker walked in.

"Ryker!" Natazhia screamed as she launched off the bench where she was sitting and ran toward him. Her momentum caused him to stumble as she threw her arms around him and had he not been able to brace himself with a hand from Grayson, they'd have both hit the floor.

"Whoa, honey! I'm not complaining," he said, his eyes twinkling as he smiled, "but it's only been a few hours."

Breathlessly, Natazhia stammered. "I know, I know, it's just that, it's, I mean, I was so worried for you and the kids—wait, the kids—where, I mean, did you find them?"

Ryker glanced at Zyra who gave him a stern look; Natazhia looked up at him, confused by the eye contact.

"Shhh," he whispered, "I'll tell you everything, just not right now."

Tears now streaming down her face, Natazhia questioned him. "But?"

Still whispering, but harshly, Ryker said, "NOT HERE, NOT RIGHT NOW. Come on, walk, let's sit down."

As they all sat down, Zyra addressed the forty. "I trust your bellies are full and that you've all rehydrated," she started.

But Natazhia couldn't focus on her words. It was as if she was at the bottom of a swimming pool, barely able to distinguish what those outside of it were saying. She could only hear her own thoughts. *What is Ryker not telling me? Oh God, I hope nothing happened to them. Are they okay?* She couldn't stop herself from feeling guilty. *I promised Blaise I'd be home as soon as I could; I shouldn't be here. I should have left Ryker and gone back home to them. But you'd be dead,* she argued with herself.

"Natazhia." Ryker nudged her and said, still whispering, "Pay attention. This is important."

Letting her thoughts go, Natazhia tried to pay attention as Zyra continued.

"We weren't able to hold them off any longer at the borders. Now that they've convinced our former comrades in the east to join them, the Republic is stronger and has more firepower. We must stay underground until the Liberation believes they've captured and arrested everyone."

Natazhia stood up. "Aren't we leaders? Are you saying we hide down here like cowards while our friends, our families, our neighbors die at the hands of the Liberation?"

Ryker pulled at her sleeve and whispered, "Sit down, Natazhia."

Swiftly turning, Natazhia glared down at her husband, unused to him telling her what to do, and uttered through clenched teeth, "I will not sit and do nothing while our children are out there!"

"Are the two of you done bickering so I can answer your question and we can move on?" Zyra asked, her voice dripping with sarcasm.

Natazhia felt her face get red hot as she blushed, and she fought back the tears welling up again, refusing to show weakness in front of Zyra. "We are," she said as she shot another look at Ryker, almost daring him to speak up.

He shrugged his shoulders and put his hands up, shaking his head, and the others laughed.

Natazhia felt her face heat up again but turned to look at Zyra, who was staring back, with her head cocked slightly to the side and her hand on her hip.

"Natazhia," Zyra said, "do you *really* want an answer, or was your question more about your ego and your need to stand on a higher pedestal than mine?"

Natazhia was angry as she said, "I don't need a pedestal, but since you seem to be the one in charge here, why are we hiding rather than fighting?"

"Let me ask you something, Natazhia," Zyra said. "Do you have the benefit of a network of Rebel Intelligence providing you with troop movement, weapon count, and potential targets?"

Natazhia started to respond, but even before she made a sound, Zyra interrupted her.

"Of course, you don't, so how about you take a big risk and trust that my leadership team and I have the best interests of the citizens and the rebels at heart with every decision. I know, it's a lot to ask, but considering the provisions for you and your family, I think you could at least try." Zyra turned away from Natazhia and spoke to the rest of the room. "As I was saying, over the next few weeks, months, or, perhaps longer, we will be conducting intense training to prepare each of you for the roles you will assume once the fighting ceases and the Reformed Liberation of America (the RLA) is powerless. In a few moments, Allen will take you to the living quarters and give you instructions on where and when to meet tomorrow. Cooked breakfast isn't available in the morning, so please allow yourself time to ensure you've eaten and hydrated. Allen will answer any questions during your tour of the campus on the way to your living quarters."

Zyra looked over at Ryker and nodded her head toward the door.

Ryker stood up, kissed Natazhia on the forehead, and said, "I'll see you shortly, and I promise, I'll explain everything; it will all make sense. I promise."

She reached for his hand and pulled as if to stop him, then just gave him a gentle squeeze and smiled. Letting go of his hand, she kissed her first two fingers and held them up toward Ryker as he turned to go.

Allen called out to them. "All right, y'all, I know everyone's tired, and we've got a lot of ground to cover yet before we get to your living quarters and you can get some shut-eye."

As if I could sleep when Serenity, Jacob, and Blaise are still out there. Natazhia stood up and followed, bringing up the rear once again. As she approached the door, she saw Racyne and Tristen standing on the other side of the threshold, waiting for her. *What do these two want now?* Natazhia was not used to being around anyone outside of her family. Socializing with others was so far outside her comfort zone that she was uncomfortable spending so much time with the two women who had awkwardly befriended her. *Smile,* she said to herself, *you only need to be friendly for a little bit longer.*

"What's going on, chicky?" Racyne asked. "Did your husband tell you anything more than Zyra said in there?"

"No, nothing," Natazhia answered, looking at the tiled floor as she walked.

"What do you mean, nothing?" Tristen, prodding, said, "He's been with them all day. How can he not know anything?"

"Look, he couldn't even tell me if my kids are dead or alive. When I say nothing, I mean nothing," Natazhia answered impatiently. "If he can't answer that much for me, I really could care less what else he might know."

"Hey, sorry to ask," Racyne said, then paused a moment before continuing. "Ya know, I may not have kids and all that, but you at least have him down here with you. Doug is out there somewhere, and I don't even think you bothered asking who Tristen had to leave behind. So, could you maybe quit treating everyone like you're the only one who lost someone?"

"Oh, man, I'm sorry, guys. You must think I'm a real jerk. I know. I am so grateful Ryker is here with me now. The kids, I just don't know how to explain it. My mom tried before I had my own, and well, it's just not something you can fully grasp until you hold them in your arms that first time. The thought that they are gone, or suffering, or even that they are safe at home alone and scared, not knowing if and when we are coming back, it's like having the wind knocked out of you, and you're gasping for air, but it won't come. And the only thing that will fill your lungs again is more than that one breath, what you need is to see just one smile, or a touch from one of their little hands, anything to give you hope." Natazhia sighed deeply. "But not knowing if that will ever happen again, it's just hard to breathe, let alone think about saving the world."

"Gosh, Natazhia," Tristen said, her eyes widening. "Do you think my parents ever felt that way about me? You know, before the Liberation killed them?"

"Yeah, sure they did, Tristen," Natazhia said. "There's no love like the love between a mother and her child; it's unending. Time and space can't change it."

"You say that, but I was a disappointment to mother. I didn't like guys, and so as far as they were concerned, I stood for everything they hated. I was a reminder of the anti-Christian evil the RLA stood for. She and my dad were part of the Rebellion, and they never said it, but I know I embarrassed them."

"Tristen," Natazhia responded tenderly, "nothing changes the way a mother feels about her daughter, nothing. I'm so sorry you never got the chance to hear that from her, but she loved you. I'm sure you were the very breath she breathed, and even if she disapproved of your lifestyle, I'm sure her love for you and your freedom was why they fought." Natazhia stepped in between the two women and put an arm around each of their shoulders as they walked together. "I apologize. I know I've been difficult. You're right; I'm so blessed Ryker is here."

They followed Allen and the rest of the group into a large bay with several large thin monitors adorning the walls, couches, and oversized pillow-like chairs surrounding each one. Tables, coffee tables, and end tables splashed about the room, and to the far left was a long kitchen island with all the makings of a modern kitchen behind it.

As Natazhia took in the size and luxury of the dayroom and kitchen, she pictured the little underground storage bunker at home in contrast to the facility where she now stood. To call it a bunker didn't do it justice. Earlier in the day at the trading post, what Zyra Kim had referred to as the bunker turned out to be more a state-of-the-art compound, built entirely underground and hidden from the rest of the world.

"This, ladies and gentlemen, is your dayroom," Allen said. "The kitchen has everything you need; there's a coffee and espresso bar and groceries for breakfast, lunch, or dinner. The staff will check it daily and replenish anything that's low. If it's not in there, it's not something we get, so don't bother asking."

Racyne looked at Natazhia and raised her eyebrow. Natazhia snorted, trying to hold back her laughter.

"Did someone have a question?" Allen asked, standing up on his tippy toes and peering over the heads in front to determine where the noise originated.

The three of them were shaking uncontrollably to keep the sound from escaping their lips. It had been a long day, and for whatever reason, Allen's professor-like mannerism coupled with Racyne's reaction had struck a chord in each of them, and they found it hard to control their laughter.

"Was there a question? I'm sure I heard something. Hmmm, it must have been one of those packrats I saw the other night," Allen said, winking at the three of them as a few of the other women squealed and looked around. They couldn't help it, and all three burst out into laughter. It felt so good just to let out all of the tension of the day for a few brief seconds.

"All right, LADIES and gentlemen," he said, emphasizing the word ladies for their benefit, "to your left, there's a hallway. You each have your own rooms and bathrooms. You'll find your name on the door. Inside the desk, you'll find an electronic tablet and your scan bracelet, which will serve as your identification and provide entry and exit to all areas of the compound you are authorized to access. There's also a stylus for writing on the tablet. You need to bring your tablet and stylus to the training arena, where we spent the first several hours together, by 8:30 am. The doors will open at 8:15 am, and they will close at 8:30 am. I trust you understand what happens when they close."

The room filled with murmurs as everyone recalled what had happened earlier in the day when the doors closed. Natazhia found it hard to focus on Allen's instructions. While it had been a long day, it didn't seem long enough for anyone to manage all the logistics that had Allen described. She wondered just how many people were already down here. They must have known about and prepared in advance for the attack.

"Okay, settle down," said Allen. "I take it then that EVERYONE will be in their seats at 8:30 tomorrow morning. Great, you each have six sets of uniforms in your closets. Tomorrow, you will wear the olive uniform. Your bathroom has robes, towels, and toiletries. Our staff maintains your rooms should you run low on anything." Allen paused, looking around at the group. "Well then, unless there are questions, have a good night."

Everyone started down the hall looking from left to right at the doors for their names. Not feeling up to peopling any longer, Natazhia flopped down in one of the pillow-like chairs. She thought she'd wait for the halls to clear out a bit after everyone else found their rooms.

"Hey Natazhia," Racyne called, "aren't you going to bed?"

"I'll look in a minute once everyone's found their rooms. No sense in tripping over one another."

"Okay, it's your call!" Racyne said, as she began to walk down the hall, looking at name labels beside each door. "Flynn, right? Are you Natazhia Flynn? Your room is here on the left."

"Hey, thanks! Yes, it's Flynn." *How'd I end up right at the front of the hall?* Natazhia wondered as she stood up, sooner than she had wished. *Darn, I was comfortable.* She walked over to the hallway to the first door on the left and looked at the label, "Flynn." She turned the handle and walked in the door, exhausted and ready for sleep. Closing the door behind her, shrieking voices startled her, followed by the pounding footsteps of Jacob, Blaise, and Serenity all rushing toward her, calling out, "MOM!" The children knocked her off balance as they all hugged her at once. Ryker stood in the center of the room, smiling.

"Oh, my goodness, I can't believe it. You're okay! But how? What happened?"

The twins talked over one another, each getting louder and louder.

"Ssshhh! The others will hear us for sure."

Ryker laughed. "Nope, as I understand, these quarters are as soundproof as you can get, so they can make all the noise they want." He paused, just as the boys began to scream louder, then raised his voice for emphasis. "Within reason!"

They all laughed.

"Mommy, come see our bedroom!" Blaise grabbed Natazhia's hand and led her through the room to a short hallway with four additional doorways. "That's our bathroom," he said, pointing as they walked past it to the door directly in front of them. "This room is for Jacob and me. See our closet, Mommy! They put new clothes in there for us! They are all the same! I don't know how they will ever tell us apart when we wear the same gray color every single day! Serenity has them too! Her uniforms are gray just like ours, only way bigger! Look, two separate beds! I don't have to climb up top anymore, so I can't jump and make you scared I'm going to get hurt. But Daddy said I don't have to worry about that anymore because people here don't care if I'm extra."

Puzzled, Natazhia said, "Oh honey, you're not extra. You're everything we ever wanted and perfectly you." Looking up at Ryker, she said with concern, "What do you mean he doesn't have to worry? We can't trust these people."

Ryker smiled. "Let's get the kids to bed, and I'll explain everything."

Natazhia put her arm around Serenity. "I imagine it's been quite a day for you?"

"Yeah, Mom, it's kinda been a roller-coaster, but Dad and Mr. Doyle got to us before Mrs. Johnson had a nervous breakdown. When we walked in the house, and she saw Blaise and Jacob in the same room, she lost it."

"What, Letty knows?" Natazhia asked nervously while looking at Ryker.

"Yep, she will probably never let you hear the end of when she sees you," Serenity said.

"I do hope I'll see her again, even if she does let me have it."

"Why wouldn't you, Mom?" she asked. "She's here, along with her family. Mr. Doyle found out she was a school teacher and asked them to come with us. He said the other kids here need a good teacher, too."

"Really? Letty, her family. Wait! Are there other kids? But how? No one came in with children." Natazhia looked at Ryker. "What is happening? I don't understand."

"I promise, I'll explain everything. It's been a long day for all of us," Ryker said. "Let's get these little ones tucked in and then we can talk."

"Let's everyone say prayers together tonight," Jacob piped in.

"Hey dude," Ryker responded, "that's a great idea. Come on, everyone, let's gather in."

Together they chanted, "Now I lay me down to sleep; I pray the Lord my soul to keep. If I die before I wake, I pray the Lord, my soul, to take. Amen." They hugged and kissed one another, tucked the boys in bed with kisses, and Natazhia followed Serenity to her room.

"I miss our home, Mom," Serenity confided, "but I'm really grateful we are all together and that we are all safe. I'm glad the Johnsons were allowed to come with us, too. But Dad wouldn't let me bring Hattie."

"Awe, Serenity," Natazhia said, running her fingers through her daughter's long hair, "I'm going to miss Hattie, too. And, I'm so grateful Daddy and Commander Doyle found you three safe and sound and brought you to me. I don't know what I would do without my girl. I love you." She kissed her daughter on the cheek, drew a cross on her forehead, stood, and walked out of the room, pulling the door to as she did. She walked past the room the boys were in and peeked through the small door opening Ryker had left, and finally let out a sigh of relief, grateful her family was alive and safe.

Natazhia turned away from the door and took a step only to discover her husband was standing directly behind her. She looked up as he wrapped his arms around her, and just as she started to speak, Ryker shook his head. "Shhh, no more questions tonight," he murmured and covered her lips with his mouth, kissing her. Although she wanted answers, Natazhia allowed herself to melt in his arms and returned his kiss. She followed him to the bedroom, letting her questions about his day and all that would come tomorrow slip away. She was determined to savor every second of the present after many tense hours of uncertainty and fear she'd never hold her husband again.

6

PSYCHOLOGICAL WARFARE

Natazhia awoke to the sound of an alarm that filled the entire compound. The loud, persistent beeping, reminiscent of an old alarm clock, startled her as she shot up in her bed, heart racing even when a pleasant voice replaced the alarm and announced over the loudspeaker, "A pleasant morning to all of our new guests. At this time, please prepare for your day. The school will begin promptly in one hour. Please drop off all children under the age of eighteen to Zone B-2058. I repeat, all children under age eighteen must be at Zone B-2058 fifteen minutes before the hour. Thank you, and have a pleasant day."

Ryker hadn't even moved. *I don't understand how this man sleeps through every noise, yet he'll complain he didn't get any sleep when he wakes up.* Natazhia, now calmer, grew more frustrated trying to wake Ryker. *Forty-five minutes to get the kids to school is going to be difficult. How will we continue to hide one of the boys?* Natazhia and Ryker had fallen asleep without an explanation from Ryker regarding the recovery of her children.

"What? What?" Ryker groggily asked when he finally responded to her nudges.

"I can't believe you didn't hear all of that."

Just then, the alarm began blaring again, and the pleasant voice followed it. "Attention Guests, this is a reminder that you are to return to the meeting hall in one hour and ten minutes. Please allow me to remind you, the doors to the meeting hall shall close in exactly one hour and ten minutes."

Natazhia hopped off the bed and rushed to the boys' bedroom. As she stepped in the doorway, the lights gradually brightened. "Blaise, Jacob! It's time to wake up! Hurry!" Then she walked to her daughter's room, and again, the lights gradually increased in brightness as she entered.

"I'm awake, Mom!" said her daughter before Natazhia said anything.

"Okay, well, hurry up and get dressed and help me with your brothers," she said, turning to leave the room and talking to no one in particular as she continued back to her room. "I've still got to figure out how to keep one hidden here."

"We don't have to hide either of them here," Ryker said. "Both boys can go to school every day."

"How can you be so sure, Ryker?" she asked. "Something just doesn't feel right about this, or even about any of what happened yesterday."

"Honey, I know, just trust me, they are safe. I promise I'll find some time to explain everything." He gave his wife a reassuring hug. "I spent the entire day with Grayson; he needs us. The safety of the children is his top priority."

"Ryker, it's not that I don't trust you, or Grayson for that matter," she said and then explained further. "It's just, well, there was this man at the fabric tent. It was almost as if he knew something terrible was going to happen. He made me feel uneasy, and I can't explain why. I just know he's connected somehow."

"We will talk later," Ryker responded, pulling on a black uniform, similar to the ones the boys had shown her the night before, "I promise. But right now, let's get a move on to the kitchen and feed these kids before school. We don't want them late on their first day."

Natazhia nodded her head. "Okay, yes." Quickly brushing her hair, she said, "And I don't want to be late to the gathering hall."

Puzzled, Ryker looked at her and offered his help. "Get yourself ready. I'm not meeting Grayson until a little later. So, I'll drop the kids off to give you some extra time."

A few minutes later, Ryker and Natazhia gathered the children to go to the community kitchen and make their breakfasts. As the family stepped out of their room and Natazhia closed the door behind them, she was acutely aware of a sudden halt in the talking and commotion. She felt all eyes on the family of five as they walked through the dayroom to the kitchen. The reaction of her peers shook her confidence in Ryker's reassurance that the children would be okay.

"Mama," Serenity whispered as she grabbed her mother's arm and pulled her in as close as she could, "why are they staring at us like that? They seem so angry."

Natazhia wanted desperately to reassure her daughter, and at the same time, she was frightened too. Serenity was right; they seemed angry. "Honey, I'm sure they're just surprised. Besides, they've probably never seen identical twins before." Instinctively, she reached back for the boys and pulled them closer to her.

As they approached the kitchen, she saw Racyne standing behind the counter with a coffee cup in hand, her jaw dropped and mouth wide open, watching as the family approached. Realizing that she was staring, Racyne shifted into a big smile and nearly spilled her coffee as she quickly put down her cup and stepped around the counter to greet them.

"Oh, my goodness," she shrieked, squatting down to get closer to the boys, "Natazhia, are both of these handsome little men yours? But how? You didn't tell me there were three. How have you been? Never mind, just let me get a good look at them. I heard that people used to have identical twins, but, oh gosh, they are just amazing."

Natazhia stood by uncomfortably as her new friend fawned over her boys, who loved the attention. The others began to gather around, poking them and commenting to one another as if the boys were caged animals at the zoo.

"Coming through, make a hole!" Tristen moved through the crowd. "Come on, everybody, break it up, break it up!"

Natazhia never imagined she'd do anything more than tolerate Tristen; however, at the moment, she'd never been so grateful for anyone's friendship.

"Haven't you ever seen twins before?" She gasped as she broke through the group and came face to face with Natazhia's family. "Well, okay, I guess no one's ever seen them in real life," she said after regaining her composure. "But since they are real life and we're on a schedule, back off and let them eat!" She smiled at the boys. "So, whatcha eatin'? Can I get you something?"

Natazhia was relieved to see the crowd disperse, and she was grateful for Tristen's friendly offer. However, they were running out of time. "It's going to have to be something fast, boys," she interjected. "You only have a few minutes before you need to be at school."

"Nutrition bars it is, then," Tristen said.

"What's that?" Blaise asked inquisitively.

"What do you mean, what's that?" Tristen chided. "Haven't you ever had one? Y'all been living under a rock, or what?"

The boys shrugged their shoulders, and they each took one as Tristen pulled them out of the basket on the countertop and handed them the wrapped bars. She tossed one to Natazhia and then gave her a cup of coffee. "It's black. Did you want anything in it?"

"No, thank you," she replied, bringing the cup to her lips.

"No time, bring it with you; we gotta get a move on, especially if you don't want me pushing you out of the way again," Racyne said, smiling with their inside joke. "Where's your tablet and bracelet?"

Natazhia realized in her rush to get the kids out of the room, she left everything behind. "I'll be right back. I can catch up."

Tristen objected. "No, we stick together today. Hand me your coffee; I'll hold it for you while you run back to your room."

She opened her mouth to argue, then recalled the conversation in the meeting room yesterday and decided it was better not to. "Okay, I'll hurry." Natazhia gave her husband and kids, a quick peck on each cheek, then ran back to their room, calling over her shoulder, "I'll see you all later! Ryker, thanks for getting them to class on time!"

Once in the room, Natazhia opened the desk drawer where she'd left the bracelet, tablet, and stylus the night before. She grabbed the messenger bag from the top of the dresser next to the desk and hastily stuffed in the tablet, stylus, and nutrition bar her friend gave her. As she reached in, she felt the familiar leather of her mother's Bible and let out a gasp as relief washed over her. *But how? Ryker of, course.* Smiling, then she looked at the bracelet, and when she started to put it on her wrist, the stones began to glow. *What is that all about? How does this thing work?* Instinctively, she changed her mind and tossed it in the bag with her other belongings. Another surprise was seeing her leather jacket hanging on a hook near the door. She was more than grateful for its return and quickly shoved it in the bag.

The kitchen was nearly empty except for Byron and a few others when Natazhia returned to join her friends.

"You ready?" Racyne asked as Tristen handed the coffee back to Natazhia.

"I think so," she said breathlessly. "What do you think we're in for today?"

"Oh, I don't know," Racyne answered. "More of the same, I suppose."

As the three women were heading out of the kitchen, Natazhia noticed that Byron and the others didn't appear to be in any hurry to leave. Preferring not to repeat yesterday's topic of conversation, she called over her shoulder, "Byron, you guys coming?"

"Uh, yeah, we've got time still," he called back.

Natazhia stopped and looked back at the group. "I don't think so; it's a bit of a walk. Why don't you guys hurry on up and come with us?"

One of the women answered for him. "We can manage. We'd rather not be associated with an infidel."

Instantly, Tristen and Natazhia looked ready for a confrontation, so Racyne put a hand on each of their shoulders. "Not now, ladies.

Let's get to the room on time. It can wait. We need to hurry; we don't want to be late."

As the women hurried along together toward the doors, Natazhia said, "What did she mean? Who was she calling an infidel?"

Tristen and Racyne glanced at one another knowingly but didn't say anything. Their friend didn't seem to notice, so Racyne responded. "Let's not worry about it right now; we gotta scoot." The two of them picked up speed, and Natazhia followed, replaying the conversation in her head in an attempt to figure out what the woman meant.

As the three approached the end of the hall where the gathering room was, they joined the end of the line for the entry. Standing on her tiptoes, Natazhia could see that the doors were still closed. "What time is it?" she asked no one in particular.

The woman in front of them looked at her bracelet and started to answer as she turned around. "Eight—uh—" followed by a long sigh, rolling her eyes, turning her back on Natazhia, and facing the doors again.

"I'm sorry," Natazhia said, "I didn't hear that."

"It's eight-twenty-four." Racyne answered for the woman in front of them. "Eight-twenty-four," she said again.

"What am I missing here?"

"Natazhia, you have three children—" Tristen said. "No living person that anyone knows has three children, and this morning you paraded them in front of everyone as though it was nothing." She continued. "Give everyone some time to process; I'm sure it will pass."

"So, Byron and the others?" Natazhia stopped mid-question. *But Ryker said we were safe here. How could he have misjudged the situation?*

"It's really getting close to 8:30," Tristen said nervously, checking the time on her bracelet again. "I hope they're going to give us enough time to get in there and sit down."

Natazhia stepped out of line to see if Byron and the others had arrived yet. Not seeing them, she looked back at her friends and said, "Hey Tristen, Racyne, I'm gonna go look for Byron; he's still not here."

"Natazhia, no!" Racyne said. "Let me go. You'll only make it worse!"

"What do you mean, I'll make it worse? I'm just going to go look for them. I don't want Byron getting called to the carpet again."

"Look, I know you want to help," Racyne said, "and you can. It's just best if you do so by keeping yourself out of the spotlight for now. Trust me. I'll go." She smiled. "Besides, my legs are a lot longer than yours, and I'll cover more ground quicker. Get back in line and stay with Tristen."

Natazhia's eyes welled up with tears of frustration. *All I wanted was for Ryker and me to do what was right, and now it seems nothing I do is right.* She stood quietly with Tristen doing her best to hide her emotions while Racyne headed back to the kitchen. The line started moving slowly ahead. "What time is it?"

Tristen said, "Where's your bracelet? It looks like you'll need it to get in. It's 8:28."

"It's in my bag. I, uh, I don't like anything on my wrist." She was about to confess she didn't trust the electronic device but decided she'd better keep her concerns to herself for the time being. She pulled the bracelet out of her bag and held it as the line inched forward. *Come on, people, let's move it.* She thought to herself, recalling Paul's words from yesterday. It seemed like a lifetime ago. *Was that only yesterday?* When she looked at the bracelet to see how much time they had left to get in the room, she saw that it was blank. "Mine doesn't show the time. I think something's wrong with it."

"You have to put it on," her friend answered matter-of-factly. "It uses energy from your body somehow to charge it and only works when you're wearing it."

Natazhia recalled the conspiracy theories she'd heard as a child about how some electronics created a kind of artificial intelligence nanotechnology that could sync with human DNA and become part of the brain. She wondered if the bracelets were that kind of artificial intelligence. She could see that those ahead of her were scanning their bracelets to enter the room. Grasping hers tightly in her hand, she hoped it would charge that way, but it remained dark with no sign of life. She and Tristen were getting closer to the door when she heard Professor begin the countdown.

"Thirty, twenty-nine, twenty-eight—"

Natazhia stepped away from the line just enough to look back for Racyne and saw her and the others running down the hallway toward them. "Hurry, Racyne!" she yelled, "only twenty-five seconds." The group began to run faster. Satisfied they'd make it in the room, she turned and began moving forward with the line.

"Twenty, nineteen—" Allen was right next to her counting down the seconds. He stopped briefly to address her directly. "It won't work unless you put it on; hurry up, you're running out of time."

Natazhia felt her heart race. *But what if it's always like this? We've been in hiding all these years so the children wouldn't have to—* She reached the door; and then everyone from behind was pushing past her and interrupted her thoughts—it was time to act.

"Natazhia, let's go, hurry up! What are you doing?" Tristen cried out.

Natazhia slipped the bracelet on without thinking any more, and as she did, she felt it conform to her wrist. A warm sensation moved through her arm as the stones shifted from green to gold to blue. Then, as she stepped through the doorway, they again became a green color. She heard the familiar AI voice state her name, "Natazhia Flynn," as she entered the room.

"Nine, eight, seven—"

She could still hear Professor out in the hallway calling out the time.

"Come on, Natazhia, we have to sit down," Tristen said urgently.

The room suddenly erupted into chaos, much like the previous day. Natazhia could hear names being called out by the soothing AI voice of each person entering the room. As she approached an empty seat in the back row, someone sat down before she could get to it. She looked for another open seat near the back but could only see one near the front. She made her way to it and sat as she heard the voice call out, "Racyne Brenner, Byron Shields, Joy O'Doherty." Natazhia sighed with relief, knowing her friend must've been one of the last to enter the room. She assumed everyone had made it in as she heard the voice repeating, "Securing Entry Immediately," accompanied by an obnoxious beeping sound and followed by a loud thud, the sound of the heavy doors locking.

Tallia stood at the front of the room next to Paul on their elevated platform, her face clearly expressing disgust as she looked around the room. Several of the forty were still jockeying for seats. Tallia put her bracelet near her mouth and said something. The all-too-pleasant voice that now made Natazhia feel uneasy was audible over the ensuing chaos.

"The following personnel have not yet arrived and are considered missing, Devon Green, Hailey Johnson, Lauren McKnight."

Everything stopped. With impatience, Tallia sat down near the back of the platform, crossed her legs, and then crossed her arms. Her body language spoke a thousand words. Those who were left standing found seats quickly and sat down as quietly as they could.

"Well, what happened today that everyone didn't arrive as scheduled?" Tallia said as a general question to the group in the room. She turned to Paul. "I'm curious to hear what could have prevented them today, aren't you?"

"Absolutely! I forgot to bring the popcorn, though," he said, grinning.

The tension in the air was thick. If it was possible, it seemed to be even worse than it was the day before. Natazhia could feel her heart pounding in her chest. *This is crazy. Why am I so afraid of this woman and what she thinks?*

"Professor," Tallia said, her tight voice interrupting Natazhia's thoughts, "is there anyone outside the door?"

"Yes, Tallia. There are three team members outside."

"Very well, would you be so kind as to poke your head out and ask them to wait there? Paul will deal with them momentarily. Then come back in and grab your seat." She raised her wrist toward the doors, and as the black stones turned green, the doors opened.

Natazhia looked down at her wrist. The stones were black except for a bright flashing white light on the one that showed the time. As she stared at it, she realized that the light was pulsating at the same pace as her heartbeat. She tried to put the bracelet and its stones out of her thoughts. It made her nervous. *Do Tallia and the others know what I'm thinking and feeling because I'm wearing the bracelet? I wonder if anyone else thinks the way I do, or am I just paranoid?*

Professor came back into the room and pulled up a seat next to the closed doors.

Tallia stood up and walked toward the front of the platform, and stepped down onto the floor of the room. She walked halfway down the center aisle between the two sides of the room, taking her time to make eye contact with each person whose eyes followed her as she surveyed the room before turning around and walking back toward the front. With her back still toward everyone, she said, "What I don't understand is, why, after everything we've already been through together, three of your team didn't matter to you enough to ensure they were in the room?" Then, facing them all, she pointedly asked her question. "Do any of you have an explanation?"

Silence was the response of the forty to her question. Natazhia looked down at her wrist again. She watched as the secondhand on the center stone flashed with each second that went by. The silence was deafening, and it continued for several minutes. *Someone, say something,* she screamed inside her head. *What could I possibly share? I wasn't late, and I put this stupid thing on even though I didn't want to, so that I wouldn't be late. Heck, I was even willing to risk being late myself to go after them. I wonder if they were with Byron back in the kitchen?* Lost in her ruminations, Natazhia could hear the sound of voices but wasn't aware of what was said until someone speaking her name interrupted her thoughts.

"Natazhia, is that what happened? Natazhia!" Tallia said much louder a second time.

"What?" Natazhia asked, startled by the question. "Did what happen?"

"Byron claims that it was you and your children that kept the others from arriving on time."

Indignantly, Natazhia said, "That's ridiculous! Ryker and the kids left for school before we did. We asked the ones still in the kitchen to come with us. We told them they didn't have much time, but ummm—" She scanned the room. "The woman with the red hair must be one of the ones outside. Anyway, they refused; they said they had time. She said she couldn't be associated with an infidel. I tried to question them. Racyne and Tristen convinced me to let it go. I noticed they weren't in line and was going to go back for them. Racyne did instead. Heck, I even stepped back out of line before coming in to see all of them running and called out the time for them. I thought they'd make it. If they'd have left when we asked them to, they would have. The only reason he is here is that Racyne went back for them," she said, looking over at Byron, nodding her head in his direction.

"Interesting," Tallia said slowly. "Paul, what do you think? Is it possible that both of them are correct in their perspective and yet, neither is responsible?"

"Hey, that's not fair! I tried to be responsible," Natazhia said, standing up to make her point, "and I invited them to join us; I wanted to go back for them. Okay, it's possible that everyone lost track of time because they were distracted by my boys. I'm willing to take responsibility for that, but to blame me because they chose to stay in the kitchen is just plain wrong."

Paul smiled. "Natazhia, it sounds as if you took some initiative, perhaps even learned from yesterday. Why, then, does Byron feel you are responsible for their delay? You said someone referred to you and, ah, I'm sorry, who else were you with, as infidels?"

"I was with Tristen and Racyne. Um, no, I believe they were only referring to me. Or maybe them, too. But only because they were with me. I, I didn't even consider the children would upset the others," she said, stammering, "because Ryker said they were safe here, that um, we were safe. I guess this place is no different. I just, well, I hoped that maybe—" Her voice trailed off as she thought of the boys having a more normal life, and she suddenly realized that this world might never offer them that possibility. "Oh my God, the boys! I have to get them! What if? What if they are being attacked this way by the other children? By the teachers?"

"Relax, Natazhia." Paul smiled reassuringly again, and said, "They are fine. Your husband is with them and the rest of the children. We thought it best, at least for now. Go ahead and sit back down. I'll come back to you in a few."

Natazhia sat down. She kept replaying the scene from earlier that morning in her mind. *I hate that everyone treated my boys as though they were an exhibit at a zoo.* She'd dreamt of the day they could all be together with their friends and trust they were safe. *I trusted Ryker and Grayson. What on earth was I thinking? Of course, it wouldn't be okay. These people hate us!* It didn't feel safe that so many people hated the very existence of her boys. She was startled by someone yelling.

"They are criminals!"

Natazhia looked up and recognized the woman who was in front of her in the line just a few minutes earlier.

"The law says one child of each sex! They've broken the law! And now those of us who had to had to—" she began sobbing and continued, "we had to undergo the horror of—of an abortion, because, because our baby was the wrong sex, and uh, they, um, they didn't. It's, it's ju-ju-just not fair." The woman stuttered with tears flowing.

Natazhia was beginning to understand why some were angry, especially the other women. Until now, she hadn't considered that those who had experienced forced abortions and sterilization might not understand her situation. She felt the familiar guilt about her choices. She and Ryker knew they were breaking the law. But it was God's law they wanted to uphold. Her mother had taught her that abortion was murder, and she and Ryker both felt that way, too. *Will I ever be able to make them understand? I could never have done something my mother spent her entire life's mission trying to stop.*

Paul looked back toward the doors. "Professor, go ahead and let the others in now," he said. "I don't think they should miss any more of this dialogue." As Allen nodded and got up to open the doors, Paul looked at Natazhia. "Do you want to respond, Natazhia?"

"Um, I—" she paused before continuing. "Yes, I would like to."

"Very well then, would you please stand?"

Natazhia stood up apprehensively and looked over toward the woman who had been crying. "I'm so sorry, I know I, uh, I can't begin to imagine your pain. And, I'm well, I'm sorry that my boys, my children are a reminder. I want you to know, I, um, I mean, we, my husband and I, uh, we, never intended to break the law. We hadn't planned on being pregnant again. But when we were, we, uh, we discovered we had twins, and well, we just couldn't find a way to dishonor my mom. She fought so hard to stop abortion even before it became the law, and well, we, uh, I'm sorry, I don't even know how to say it, we believe there's a law that's higher than the laws of the land. We were willing to risk punishment to save the life of a human, our child. I'm so sorry that is painful for you." Reaching for the arm of her chair, she sat down.

Tallia stood up again. "Natazhia, you are not sorry."

"Yes, I am," she answered. "I'm so, so sorry."

Quietly, gently, at almost a whisper, Tallia again said, "No, Natazhia, you're not sorry. You are welcome to apologize, but you are not sorry."

Natazhia looked at her bewildered. "I don't understand."

"The word 'sorry' comes from the root 'unworthy,'" Tallia said. "You are not unworthy; in fact, none of you are unworthy. I don't want to hear you use the word 'sorry' in this room. Have I mentioned, words matter?"

Natazhia held back her tears. She felt deeply for the woman, forced in such a brutal way, to give up the life of her child. She hurt for her, yet she also cried for her children and for the sacrifices she and Ryker had made, giving up friends, disappearing without a trace from their siblings, lying to their dear friend, Letty, and her family. They'd made sacrifices, too.

Again, Paul stepped up. "Team, we have a calling to lead. To do so, we must learn to take what I like to refer to as radical responsibility. In other words, you own it, no matter what. Here, let's do this. Let's um, uh, Byron, stand up for a second."

Byron stood up; his discomfort was obvious.

Paul looked at him and said, "Byron, if you were to take responsibility for the others being late, what might that look like?"

"Well, um, I suppose, now I'm not saying everything was my fault—" Byron started.

"Of course not; this isn't about blame, but if you were responsible, radically responsible, what might you say?"

Byron paused a moment, then said, "Well, I might start with, I knew we would risk being late, and well, I chose to stay in the kitchen with the others instead of leaving when the women did because I didn't want to be perceived as an infidel, too. So, instead of putting myself in a bad light, I risked being late again, and as a result, some of the others were late."

"Excellent, Byron! How did that feel?"

"Believe it or not," he answered, face brightening, "it felt pretty good."

"So, you didn't feel blame or guilt?" Paul prodded him for more feedback.

"No, I felt—it's weird. I kinda felt empowered. I mean, I didn't own anything that wasn't mine to own, but I did take responsibility for the choices I made that contributed to the end result."

"Do you see, everyone—" Paul started walking around the room, "—that you can take responsibility without owning blame, guilt, or shame. When I suggest that you take radical responsibility, I'm not in any way suggesting you own anything that isn't yours to own. Does that make sense?"

Everyone nodded.

"Great!" Rubbing his hands together, he continued. "In a few moments, I'm going to ask you to choose a partner of the same sex. This partner will be your training partner going forward. You will be responsible for your partner. If your partner is late, you will also be late because you are responsible for ensuring your partner is on time. Got it?"

Again, everyone nodded.

"You all seem to be catching on," Paul said, nodding with them. "One by one, you will have the opportunity to pick your partner. I suggest you pick someone who challenges you, perhaps even someone you don't really like. If you truly want to become the best version of yourself as you train, that would be the path I'd recommend—or not, it's your decision. The beautiful thing is you get to choose." Paul paused to let it all sink in. "We will go around the room, and you will each pick someone and share why you chose that person. The only rules are 1) Your partner must be someone you do not already have a relationship with, and 2) Your partner should be of the same biological sex as you. And lastly, 3) You may choose to decline should someone pick you, and if you do decline, you must share why, and then pick someone else. Who'd like to start?"

After what seemed like hours of listening to the others pick their partners and share their life's story around why they chose the person they chose, Natazhia sat quietly. Still mulling over the woman's outburst and tears earlier, Natazhia was aware that neither of them had a partner yet. *How many others feel that way about me? What if I choose someone who hates me? Maybe if I just stay quiet, someone will choose me.* The longer she sat, the more convinced she became that no one was going to pick her. Natazhia scanned the room. As partners connected, they removed their chairs from the group and sat together along the edge of the room. Natazhia could see very few women left to choose from, and several of them already rubbed her the wrong way. *I've got to hurry up and pick someone before I end up with her because there's no one left.* She was pretty confident the woman wouldn't choose her. She heard the sound of clapping for two who had just agreed to be partners, and she quickly looked to determine if anyone else was going to stand up to choose a partner. Just as she started to stand, another man stood to pick his partner, so she sat back down. *It's okay; he can't choose a woman; this just gives me more time to decide.* She continued to talk herself through the choices that were left and then heard the clapping again. Nervous about what would happen if she didn't hurry, she quickly stood up.

"Okay, then, Natazhia, who would you like to select to be your training partner?" Paul asked.

Even though she decided to stand, the question caught her unprepared. Natazhia still had not committed fully to which of the four remaining women she wanted for a partner. She just knew she didn't want to be last. "Um, I'm picking Dian," she said.

Tallia said, "Tell Dian why you've chosen her."

Say something! Natazhia screamed inside her head. "Um, she looks like someone who takes care of her physical body, and I admire that," she said, knowing it was a lie.

The other woman laughed obnoxiously and feigned humility. "Oh, wow, me! Thank you for that compliment. Well, okay, I accept."

Oh God, please. You're so fake. I'm not sure what Paul thinks I can learn by picking someone I don't like, but I'm game. I'll give it a try. Natazhia quietly congratulated herself for her quick thinking. After all, the last thing she wanted to do was tell her new training partner that she picked her because Dian had gotten on every last nerve every time she spoke. *Well, at least she'll be strong enough to pair up with when we do combat training.* The remaining women were quite overweight, and Natazhia didn't want to worry about dead weight during the physical exercise mentioned the day prior.

The two women picked up their chairs and took them to the edge of the room while the others continued selecting partners. Even though they had only been in the room for a few hours, Natazhia felt drained. Fear and doubt occupied her thoughts. *Why did we come here? Wouldn't we have been better off taking our chances on our land? Ryker got to the kids and back. We could have waited it out in our bunker. Who are we to lead? Okay, Ryker, maybe; not me.* Her head was pounding, and Natazhia wanted nothing more than to go back home to the quiet of their little farm hidden by the creek. She couldn't grasp how her life had changed so drastically in just over 24 hours.

The sound of an alarm made Natazhia jump back into the present scene.

Louder than the morning wake-up alarm, the beeping was much more rapid, almost frantic. "Attention all personnel and residents! Attention all personnel and residents!" The familiar AI voice calmly repeated words over the loudspeakers. "This is NOT a drill; I repeat, this is NOT a drill." It continued with more information, mixing in with the alarm beeping and the increasing uproar in the room. "We have received information from credible sources that an attack is imminent. Please remain calm and at your present location. I repeat, please remain calm and at your present location."

While the alarm continued to sound in the background, a woman began screaming and then ran to the closed set of doors, attempting to pry one open with her fingertips. Quickly realizing her effort was useless, she called out for help and began pounding on the door.

The AI voice was still audible over the commotion growing in the room. "Attention, Security Personnel. Please prepare all occupied shelter locations for lockdown. I repeat, Attention, Security Personnel, please prepare all occupied shelter locations for lockdown." The alarm was relentless and the uproar in the room escalated quickly into chaos.

Prompted to calm down the woman who was pounding on the closed doors, Allen ran over and wrapped his arms around her from behind, constraining her in a bear hug while she struggled. He soon saw it was pointless, as others began pounding on the doors in her place with equally feeble attempts to pry them open.

Natazhia and Dian stood up beside their chairs, observing the tumult without speaking. Natazhia looked over at Tallia and Paul who still sat in their chairs on the podium, quietly talking with one another while scanning the activity in the room. Their casual demeanor was somewhat unnerving and didn't make any sense related to the chaos surrounding them. Keeping her eyes on Tallia and Paul, Natazhia raised her voice so Dian could hear above the noise. "Is this real?"

"I don't know," her partner answered. "It seems real enough; why wouldn't it be? You seem awfully paranoid."

"Who isn't anymore?" Natazhia asked. "I mean, who are any of these people? Doesn't this situation seem, I don't know, somehow off?"

Dian also raised her voice over the tumult, fueling her argumentative stance. "Zyra Kim is only the most famous rebel trainer. She's responsible for rebels who've infiltrated all levels of government, Hollywood, music, and the business sectors. I want that kind of freedom. And I want it without selling my soul to the other side. She can do that for us, for me."

"Is this freedom, though?" Natazhia said. "Really? I mean, what if living down here and being questioned about our motives in the name of preparing for some new world we never see is all that's left for us?"

"How do you justify living without hope for a better world, Natazhia?" Dian looked intently at Natazhia, wanting to know the answer. She said, "Don't those kids of yours at least deserve to believe freedom is possible?"

Natazhia felt as though she'd been punched in the gut and became immediately defensive. Her kids were her world! Who was this woman to insinuate that she treated them any less than they deserved? "Just what the hell do you know about being a mother, Dian?" she angrily fired back.

"I know enough about parenting not to bring children into the world illegally!" Dian shouted over the din.

"Really, Dian?" Natazhia's eyes flashed and her cheeks flushed. "If you know so much, tell me, you discover you have two healthy babies with beating hearts, kicking one another and holding each other, and you watch the ultra-sound screen in awe, which one do you chose to live and which one do you chose for execution?"

Dian wouldn't back down. "I don't know, Natazhia. Perhaps the choice will be clearer now that they're older! Which one will you choose for execution once someone turns you and your family into the Liberation?"

Chest heavy, heart ready to explode from beating like rapid machine gun fire, Natazhia choked on words ready to leap past the lump in her throat. Everything was a blur through tears mixed with anger and pain at even a suggestion of anyone taking the life of any one of her children. "What do you mean 'turns us in'?" she spat, her voice dripping with disdain.

"C'mon, lady!" Dian said, continuing to push her buttons. "You can't seriously be naïve enough to think everyone down here wants to fight for a free world! Those rose-colored sunglasses of yours certainly make you blind to reality! Many will turn over a big prize like your family in a heartbeat to live the cushy lifestyle the Liberation offers in turn. They don't care about the rest of us; they just came down here to save their own asses!"

"Are you one of those people, Dian?" Natazhia asked, only slightly aware that the alarms had stopped and the chaos was beginning to subside.

"No," the other woman answered quietly now that others would hear them. Looking down at her feet, she said, "I want to see freedom in my lifetime. I want to experience the kind of life my great-grandmother told me stories about."

The two women fell into exhausted silence. Natazhia leaned back against the wall and slid down to sit on the floor. She looked around the room at all the people, some in conversation and others, like her, silently sitting and taking it in, lost in their thoughts. As she scanned the faces around the room, Natazhia wondered if she and Dian were both right, that she couldn't trust any of them. Finally, her gaze settled on Tallia and Paul, perched on their pedestal together at the front of the room. Despite the commotion caused by the alarms, those attempting to pry open the doors, and the widespread panic now beginning to calm, those two sat smiling and chatting with one another as if they were catching up at a coffee shop.

Natazhia's thoughts drifted again to the man at the fabric tent, and her heart began to pound. She felt goosebumps on her skin and a deep sense of knowing that his behavior at the market was in some way connected to the out-of-place casualness she was witnessing in the two instructors. She began to scan the room again, this time looking specifically for the others in leadership roles. She could see the lead team member, Jerome, sitting near the entrance as he had been when they arrived that morning. Now, he sat carelessly on the chair, rocking back and forth on the rear legs to the beat of his fingers tapping like drumsticks on the front edge, with a massive smile on his face, his legs spread wide. With his piercing blue eyes, he was searching the room as though he were at an amusement park or a nightclub, just taking it all in. His behavior seemed out of place, given the panic and threat of an attack only moments earlier.

Part of her desperately wanted to find Ryker and try to sort through the inconsistencies she had witnessed over the past couple of days. Meanwhile, she knew there was no way she could share any of her concerns with her husband. He'd just accuse her of having an overactive imagination and of being overly suspicious; Ryker had a habit of dismissing many of her concerns, chalking them up to her lack of trust. While trust didn't come easy for Natazhia, she had learned to trust herself. She knew she'd have to get to the bottom of this situation by herself, gather more evidence as she followed her intuition, and then present it to her husband. Although Racyne and Tristen were starting to grow on her, she would have to keep her thoughts to herself until she had concrete proof that things weren't what they seemed.

Natazhia's gaze shifted enough to realize that she must have been staring at Paul. He made eye contact with her, and his smile and bright blue eyes she'd noticed before losing herself to her thoughts suddenly shifted to cold, steely gray. He acknowledged her with a curt nod, and she returned it, feeling as though he somehow knew her thoughts. Then, embarrassed that he had caught her staring, she glanced toward the back of the room only to see Holly and Professor talking to one another while looking in her direction. She locked eyes with Holly for a moment until the two of them quickly turned away from looking at her. As confident as Natazhia was that she'd get to the bottom of things, she'd have to watch her step because she was sure that some, if not all of them, had grievances aimed directly at her.

7

TIME MARCHES ON

Days and weeks wore on, each one much like the prior, with alarms blaring throughout the day and night. It seemed there was always an imminent attack, yet Natazhia never heard the sound of corresponding bombs, gunfire, or anything that offered proof they'd been under attack. Hence, she remained suspicious of Tallia and Paul and their Lead Trainers. Meanwhile, all forty made it on time daily, and that was progress. They assembled quietly and orderly five minutes or more each day before the opening of the doors.

Each day brought new exercises, all in some way designed to expose every single flaw in every person's character. There were days Natazhia was grateful for everything she was learning. Other days were more complicated, when initially she was confident that she and the team had nailed whatever assignment or test they faced, only to have the objective change. Frequently it was just the slightest suggestion that would plant a seed of doubt in a person's mind; the team member would tug on that little doubt, and like a loose string, the whole assignment would unravel. It was in those moments Natazhia's impatience would take over, and she'd lose the ability to filter her thoughts before speaking, so that any shred of tact she might have completely escaped her. Those days frustrated her more than she liked to admit. She wrestled with confusion, self-worth, and even more distrust for this "process" she and the rest of the forty were going through. The leaders said, "Trust the process," and Natazhia wanted to know where this process was taking them. Many had no trouble blindly following Tallia and Paul; some even seemed to idolize the pair and spent each day jumping through hoops in hopes of receiving some sign of approval from the instructors. The time spent in the "arena," as Tallia and Paul referred to the classroom, was long. They expected exhaustion, and their tempers often flared. Natazhia wrestled between her distrust of the entire construct and her desire to fit in and be accepted.

On the nights she had the opportunity to eat dinner with her family, Natazhia learned that Serenity, Jacob, and Blaise were doing many of the same exercises during their school days. The training was especially difficult for the boys. They'd spent their entire lives trying to behave exactly like the other so they could each keep their sibling's existence a secret. They were being encouraged to explore their individuality and their differences. It was good for them, and they also struggled with the separation. The twins' identities were intertwined, so they felt as though they were losing a part of themselves. Family dinners often became a boxing ring of verbal jabs, heated arguments, glares, and tears as the boys tried to sort through their emotions.

Serenity was often distracted by her budding social life, so she always hurried to get through dinner and leave to spend time with friends. She'd worked hard on the farm and at school her whole life. Maintaining a good work ethic had been much easier at home since there weren't nearly as many distractions. Now, at the compound, there were other teens, and some of the boys were showing interest in her.

Natazhia often found herself being too hard on her daughter. Although she just wanted Serenity to make good decisions and understand that her worth went far beyond how she looked and dressed, she could see her daughter's confidence and security slipping away as she sought to gain attention from the boys, despite their training. She observed that Serenity also felt a mounting pressure to decide how she would serve in the compound and the new world if it were ever safe to return above ground. At the farm, Serenity learned everything from sewing and shooting to medicine, gardening, and butchering. She knew she'd need all of those skills to survive. Now she was being asked to specialize and become an expert in a chosen area. While Natazhia understood the need for experts in different fields, she wanted her daughter to have the range of skills necessary to be independent.

Ryker spent more and more time with Grayson Doyle. Their focus was always on security, weapons, and the infrastructure of the compound with continuous deadlines. From what Natazhia could gather, those who worked in support roles within the compound were not necessarily taught the culture, nor had they bought into the philosophy that Zyra Kim's band of leaders required of the forty. As a result, Ryker's daily work with many of the others was outside the realm of Zyra's culture, which meant he returned to his family's cozy living quarters stressed and seeking solitude. For so long, Natazhia and the children had Ryker to themselves, so now they felt his absence, especially Natazhia.

During the days, Natazhia spent much of her time with Dian, not necessarily because she wanted to, but they structured their time in the arena to do almost everything together. Dian had begun to grow on her, and they had formed a friendship based on mutual respect and trust. Dian occasionally questioned the point of many of the exercises and was vocal about her disagreement. She also had reservations about Tallia and Paul, but not to the extent as her training partner. They'd heard rumblings about a dispute between Zyra Kim and her lead trainers. Dian felt that, while they might disagree with Zyra at times, the lead trainers were still loyal to her and the cause. Natazhia wasn't quite so sure. The lead team seemed less than impressed with Zyra and often dismissed and even mocked her when she wasn't in the room. While Natazhia remained unsure that she could completely trust Zyra, she respected her position of authority over the compound. Natazhia believed that any disrespect she felt toward Zyra was an indication of failure in her own leadership and therefore, displayed a lack of character. She struggled daily in discerning whether her doubts were from a place of intuition or a lack of trust.

Tristen and Racyne remained close to Natazhia and her children. The boys called them Aunty T and Aunt Race, giggling every time they called for Racyne, frequently emphasizing the words "aunt" and "race" differently, so the phrase took on a different meaning each time, followed by lots of laughter, back slaps, and "Get it? Ant Race?" When the women rolled their eyes, they did more to encourage the boys than anything else; Racyne loved the boys and the attention they gave her. While her new role with the boys helped to ease the pain of leaving her fiancé behind, as the days, weeks, and months ticked by, Natazhia could see that Racyne was beginning to lose hope that she would ever see Doug or her brother again.

Each evening, just before dinner, they received daily news briefings from Professor. The reports for remaining Rebellion Armies in the region were grim at best. The video clips and images Allen shared of families still living in the area were heartbreaking. Some were surrendering, and others were being taken from their homes in violent raids by Liberation Forces. Liberation propaganda had convinced citizens from all regions that turning in the whereabouts of friends and family members would earn elevated positions once they crossed over to Liberation Territory. The intel that Professor shared told a different story. Upon surrender and capture, they imprisoned families in FEMA (Federal Emergency Management Agency) camps under a temporary emergency order. Still, there were no reports of anyone leaving the FEMA camps that were scattered across each of the former states and cities.

Zyra Kim would visit the arena weekly to teach the forty the martial arts discipline of Aikido and remind them of their objective, to care for and protect themselves and their opponent. She would insist that in creating a world that works for everybody with no one left behind when the time came for them to do battle, the expectation was to bring life to that philosophy. Natazhia couldn't see how that was possible given the atrocities the Liberation continued to commit. Did they deserve any mercy and act of kindness or protection? How can one offer compassion to those who were out to destroy? Zyra constantly reminded them of a lesson they'd learned when dredging up past relationships with their parents. She claimed that people, in general, do the best they can with what they know. She believed those acting out the Liberation's orders could only behave and react based on what they knew to be true, even if it wasn't the same perspective of the forty and other of like mind. While Natazhia could wrap her head logically around the concept that at their core all people were good, and even understand it at an emotional level when it came to those she cared about, she couldn't, or maybe just wouldn't allow herself to believe it about the Liberation.

Natazhia clung desperately to that first moment she'd heard Zyra Kim speaking at the trading post. She could vaguely recall how the woman's message of hope and peace inspired her. As brief as it was, that flicker of hope felt like the flame of a wildfire that could spread across that land. In the darkness of their underground shelter, Natazhia's belief in hope had diminished to less than the spark of flint striking a lighter that was out of fuel. It took work to ignite, and somedays, she wasn't sure she wanted to make that effort. She knew that if she took the time each day to read from her Bible, that she'd likely rekindle the hope that seemed to elude her. However, she also feared allowing herself to hope again and found comfort in being satisfied with their current circumstances. The Bible remained in her messenger bag along with the tablet. Each morning, as she left the room before her family awoke, she took the bag and went out to the common area. Then, with a cup of coffee, she curled up in one of the reading chairs, intent on reading from her Bible. Before she read a scripture passage, there was always an assignment or homework for the kids she'd remember needed to be checked on first, so she would pull out the tablet and then distract herself with articles from Professor regarding current events until the room began to fill with the others.

Natazhia knew she should read from scripture, and she was especially hard on herself for not doing so. She was even aware that her daily habits, especially those first few hours she had to herself, would set her up positively or negatively for the day. One of the few things she was grateful for was all she was learning about human behavior, and more specifically, her own. She had discovered that the bracelets they wore changed colors based on commands and also in their resting state; one of the stones on the inside of each person's bracelet would glow a different color based upon the person's beingness. It measured whatever frequency her mood was emitting and allowed her to respond and "level-up" her vibration with the desired frequency to remain above the line in at least a state of courage or neutrality. In that state, the bead would glow a beautiful sky blue, deepening to shades of darker blue, purple, and pink when one experienced love and joy, eventually brightening to a red state when one experienced happiness and enlightenment. Natazhia found that except for the time she spent with her husband and children, when the bead would glow a beautiful purplish pink, her stone most often ranged from green to pale turquoise, indicating she was likely stuck somewhere between fear, desire, anger, or pride. Because she knew spending time with her mom's Bible in daily prayer and reflection would support her to move above the line and stay there more often, she noticed that the bracelet would drop into shades of amber when she chastised herself for not doing what she should do. It was incredibly eye-opening to see how her self-talk placed her into a state of anger, guilt, and shame. The training they were receiving provided the tools to shift out of that state. Still, Natazhia's mistrust for Tallia and Paul, along with the anger she felt toward the Liberation and the grief around leaving her old life behind, kept her stuck below the line in the lower frequencies.

Natazhia knew she had to make a shift. She knew something had to change. Logically, she knew her circumstances didn't have to dictate her state of being. Emotionally, she found it hard to let go of the picture of the life she thought she would have. And she did want to be at peace and experience joy in the life she was currently living. She knew it was time to intentionally shift her state and become the best version of herself she could be. Each night, as she drifted off to sleep, she committed herself to wake up even earlier the next day, create new habits, and make a change. After all, how could she possibly expect to impact the current leadership culture if she couldn't even lead herself?

8

ABOVE THE LINE

Natazhia felt a faint vibration on her wrist and could hear a chime coming from her messenger bag on the dresser. Confused at first by the new sound, she felt a rush of fear, followed by relief as she recalled that she'd set the alarm to create the new habits she'd mentally committed to the night before. She started to reach for the large bead on the front of her bracelet to initiate the "snooze" function and give herself another ten minutes of sleep. As soon as she'd done so, she recalled a lecture she'd heard many years earlier from her mom's collection of self-help audios. The speaker had said, "If you break the very last commitment you made to yourself before you went to sleep—the time you plan to wake up—before your feet even hit the floor, how can you possibly expect to keep commitments to others throughout the day?" As soon as she had the thought, she sat up and flung her legs over the side of the bed. *Not today, negative self-talk; you aren't winning today.*

She walked over to the bathroom and quietly closed the door behind her before turning on the light. Leaning over the sink, she turned on the cold water and splashed it over her face, then brushed her teeth. She pulled the uniform out of the closet for the day and found it ironic that today's color was almost the same amber color her bracelet shone at the lowest frequencies. And then the thought crossed her mind; *I wonder if that's by design. Could the color we wear affect us? Do they want us to remain in a lower state?* Natazhia looked to see the bead changing from the pale turquoise to shades of amber as she chastised herself. It would be more complicated than she thought to stop beating herself up and eradicate the shame and guilt she felt at never being good enough or doing things right. *Okay, I'll just set a goal to at least spend an hour or more above the line today and keep moving it upward. No more beating myself up; celebrate the wins no matter how often or how small.*

After dressing, Natazhia quietly left their living quarters with her messenger bag, and went to the common area. She made herself a coffee in the kitchen and then sat down in one of the comfortable armchairs. She switched on the reading lamp, and reached into the bag for her Bible. For a moment, she felt temptation to reach for the tablet instead. *You can look at that after; we are starting today differently.* She pulled out the Bible, ran her fingers over the soft, worn leather cover, and opened it, deciding to read wherever she landed. She found herself at Jeremiah 29:11. *For I know the plans I have for you, declares the Lord, plans for welfare and not for evil, to give you a future and a hope.* She had initially thought she'd spend thirty minutes or more reading, but that was enough. Natazhia felt a wave of peace wash over her and was compelled to turn her wrist to see the color of her stone and she smiled, noticing a radiant shade of hot pink glowing. She closed the Bible, then closed her eyes, hugging the Bible close to her heart, and began praying. *Thank You for showing me this passage today. Please watch over us and help me be a better person, leader, mom, and wife. God, I don't know why You spared my family, but help us live up to that. God, please give me discernment and wisdom and guide me every day. Amen.*

After her prayer, Natazhia reached into the bag again and pulled out a beautiful journal covered in bright fabric that Ryker had bought for her as a gift at the trading post while she was at the clothier's tent. She felt it was the right moment to open it; she had not felt inspired to write in all of the time they'd been underground. She pulled an ink pen from the bag and opened the journal, surprised to see her husband's handwriting inside the cover:

Natazhia,

Today, I'm grateful:

That we are amongst the forty.

That our children are safe.

That Grayson brought us back to you.

That our boys don't have to hide any longer.

That we are together as a family.

For my health.

For a chance to be a part of something really great.

For you.

For our eternal love.

For hope.

All my Love, Ryker

Tears were streaming down her face. She couldn't imagine how Ryker must've felt about the fact that she never mentioned or thanked him for the beautiful note inside of the journal. As bad as she felt about not opening the journal before now, she was also grateful that today was the day she opened it. It was the perfect moment and the perfect message. It was so thoughtful of Ryker to begin the gratitude journal for her. Before that day, she'd been telling him for months how much she missed journaling since pen and paper were so scarce. Natazhia had told him about her mother's practice of listing ten things she was grateful for that she already had and ten things to be thankful for someday. Her mother taught her to do this practice every day. *I get to add this to my new set of daily habits. Thank you, Ryker,* she thought, with an almost audible whisper. She removed the lid from the pen and began writing. At first, she found it challenging to think of things she would have one day. She wasn't so sure she could see anything beyond their current circumstances. She closed her eyes, looked up, and thought, *God, what is possible for me? For us?* Then the words began to flow.

Just as she started to close her journal, she realized that many others were beginning to gather in the kitchen and common area. She tucked it neatly back in her bag, picked up the coffee mug on the table next to her, and walked toward the kitchen.

"Hey, chica," Racyne called as she walked toward the kitchen, "looking for some of this?" She was holding up the pitcher filled with coffee and smiling at Natazhia.

Natazhia smiled too and walked toward her friend with her arm outstretched to refill her coffee cup.

"You're up early and looking radiant today!"

Natazhia laughed and tried to shrug off the compliment.

"No, seriously," Racyne continued, "something is different."

"I do feel different," Natazhia admitted.

"Well, whatever you did, it looks good on you!" her friend said. "Keep doing it."

"That's the plan," Natazhia replied with conviction. *That's the plan,* she repeated to herself with much less certainty.

Moments later, Ryker and the kids joined them in the kitchen, where they all sat at one of the tables and ate breakfast. Natazhia felt more like herself than she had in many years. For the first time since she'd entered the underground compound, she looked forward to joining the arena, excited by what she might learn that would support her new habits. *I need to sit down and set some goals.* She smiled, listening to the kids and their dad chat about the day ahead.

Dian walked up behind her and put her hand gently on her shoulder. "Hey partner, I hate to take you away from breakfast and all, but it's that time."

Startled, Natazhia turned her head and looked up. Hurriedly, she put down her fork, gathered her belongings, leaned over to each side of her, giving Serenity and Jacob each a kiss, then got up and walked around the table to kiss Blaise and finally Ryker. "I'm sorry, babe," she said after kissing him, "do you mind clearing my stuff from the table?"

Before he had a chance to answer, she rushed off and called over her shoulder, "Thank you, honey, I love you!"

Laughing, Dian caught up with her. "Slow down, girl," she said breathlessly, "we aren't late or anything."

"I guess I'm just excited to get to the arena today," Natazhia replied, also laughing.

"Who are you, and what did you do with the real Natazhia Flynn?"

"It's me, actually more me than you've probably ever experienced. I'm on a mission to have a better attitude about all of this."

"Does that mean I get to pack my sunglasses instead of dragging an umbrella around every time I'm with you?" Dian said, eyes twinkling.

Her friend's joke went completely over her head. "What's that supposed to mean?" Natazhia asked.

"Usually, you're the dark cloud in the room; today, you feel more like sunshine and rainbows!"

"Seriously?" Natazhia stopped walking. "Is that really how you see me?"

"Well, um, oh," Dian stammered, realizing she had misspoken. "I didn't mean— I don't— Well, others say—"

Seeing Dian's discomfort, Natazhia realized the question might have come across as aggressive, so she softened her tone. "Relax, Dian," she said, interrupting her friend. "That came out all wrong. I genuinely want to know. I can't fix my blind spots if I don't know they are there. I trust you. Just tell me what you think."

"Okay, you asked for it," Dian said. "Natazhia, when you are in a bad mood, you suck the energy out of the room. And when you let it out, man, look out for anyone in that path of destruction;

you're like a thunderstorm, hurricane, and tornado all wrapped up in one. Girl, you are so powerful; everyone can feel your presence the moment you enter a room. Use it for good, and if you aren't feeling it, either stay away from people or shift it. You can be a bit much. You're like a ticking bomb, and those who love you—" Dian paused, taking a breath and then exhaling. "Well, let's just say we tread carefully not to step on a land mine."

Natazhia stood there for a moment. The words she'd just heard felt like a punch in the gut; she knew they rang true. Fighting the urge to be defensive or justify her behavior, she looked at her friend and her eyes welled up with tears. "Thank you," she whispered, leaning over to hug her friend, "thank you for being honest."

Dian seemed relieved by her reaction; they each took a deep breath, turned without saying another word, and walked in silence to the arena. Natazhia replayed the conversation over and over again in her head. She knew her friend had provided her with valuable feedback. It still hurt to hear it, and she knew she had to do something to change it. While there were many reasons that she was still suspicious when it came to the bracelet, for the time being, she knew it would be her most valuable tool to improving herself and her leadership. She vowed to get her emotions under control.

9

MOUNT EVEREST

The hallway outside of the arena was quiet. The forty lined up in two rows, training partners side by side. Pairing up made it easy to determine if anyone was missing before the doors opening. By this point, one would expect that each day would be relatively routine, and occasionally they were. Even so, Natazhia felt anxious every time. She was nervous someone might be late, even though no one had been late in months, and even when no one was late, there was always a chance that Tallia would find something someone said, did, or didn't do to use as an example of a failure in leadership or character. Natazhia tried staying under the radar, especially now that the animosity toward her and her family had subsided.

"I still hate this part," Natazhia said in a whisper, leaning in to her partner.

"Me too," replied Dian.

The doors opened, and everyone filed in and took their seats. They all looked around, ensuring everyone was inside.

The configuration of the room was different. Chairs lined the outside of the space along the walls except for the behind the platform. In all the months they'd been there, it was the first time Natazhia had seen the room configured this way, and she wondered what was in store for them. She was confident it wouldn't be long until she found out.

"Good morning!" Tallia interjected her thoughts into the group. "Welcome to your arena today!" She continued cheerfully. "We will start the day off with a little geography and history lesson." She stepped off of the platform and began to walk along the perimeter of the room. "There was a time before most of you were even born when people traveled freely from one state to another throughout what was once known as the United States; they traveled across oceans and borders to other continents and countries."

Natazhia glanced around the room in an attempt to see how the others were reacting. She thought for sure everyone knew this part of history and wondered why Tallia would assume they didn't. It appeared the vast majority were hanging on to every word she said.

"One of the places thousands would visit was what was known as the world's deadliest mountain. Located in the Mahalangur range of the great Himalayas, on the borderline of what was once known as Nepal and Tibet in the southern part of Asia, it stands higher than any other mountain at 8,848 meters."

The lights began to dim in the room, and Natazhia noticed a definite drop in temperature; then, a holographic image of a massive snow-covered mountain appeared in the center of the room.

Tallia continued as though nothing had changed. "This mountain, known as Mount Everest, was also referred to by either its Tibetan name of Chomolungma meaning 'mother goddess of the universe,' or its Nepalese name of Sagarmatha, meaning 'goddess of the sky.' Each year approximately four hundred people would reach its summit. One in twenty-nine of them would die along the way. The trek to the summit was the ultimate physical and mental test. One that required training and a willingness to die."

The temperature in the room continued to drop, and Natazhia could feel the air in the room moving.

Tallia continued. "You all have been training for months. Paul and I have watched as you've mentally and physically prepared yourself, and we feel that today—"

Paul interrupted Tallia. "Are you sure today?"

"Yes, for most—"

"Most?"

"Yes, most. Statistically speaking, one in twenty-nine are never really prepared, despite their efforts."

"Okay, Tallia, I'll give you that—" Paul grinned. "Proceed."

"Are you sure, Paul?" she quipped back.

He nodded.

Again, turning to the forty, she said, "We feel that today you are ready, should you choose in, to take the ultimate test. Together, with Paul and I, along with your lead team, you will have the opportunity to climb Mount Everest."

The room erupted with conversation and questions.

Paul raised his hands and his voice. "Quiet, everyone. I know you have questions." He paused while the sound level decreased, then continued. "Let us explain the logistics, what it will look like, and how we will attain success. And then, if you still have questions, we will answer them one at a time. Fair enough?"

The others Natazhia could still see, not blocked from her view by the immense mountain that had appeared in the room, were nodding in agreement.

"Okay, great!" Paul continued. "Here's how the day is going to go down. First and foremost, your safety is your responsibility. You are responsible for your safety. Everyone gets that, right? Who's responsible for your safety?'

A chorus of "I am" filled the room.

"Right, you are!" Paul said. "Keep safety in the forefront of your minds. Especially since it is going to be cold, and at times you will require oxygen due to the elevation. Underneath your seats, you will find all of the gear required for your ascent."

Natazhia, Dian, and the others bent over to look under their seats, just as Paul said emphatically, "Wait for my direction on when you can reach under the seat to remove and inspect your gear."

They all sat back up as if they were six years old and caught with their hands in the cookie jar.

Paul smirked and said, "Once you have your gear in your hands, please inspect it for any sign of damage, rips, tears, or anything else that might cause it to fail. After examining the gear from below your seat, please exchange it with your partner and await the next set of instructions."

There were audible gasps throughout the room. Natazhia turned her wrist slightly to look at the bead, careful not to allow Dian to see, as she felt a familiar pit in the bottom of her stomach. Just as expected, she saw the familiar lime green shade indicating fear and anxiety. *Why do I find it so hard to trust?*

Tallia must've read her mind because she interrupted the gasps and whispers. "Hold up, everyone," she said louder than usual. "Just stop and notice what's going on for you. What have you made it mean? Paul simply asked you to inspect the gear and exchange it with your training partner, then await further instructions. Would someone like to explain what has you all so concerned about what Paul said?"

Byron spoke up immediately. "Yes, I'm bothered that you keep emphasizing that our safety is our responsibility, and then you tell us to inspect the equipment and give it to our partner. How is my safety my responsibility if I give the gear that I inspected to someone else and I wear gear someone else inspected?"

"Wow, Byron! That's a lot to unpack," Tallia said, nodding. "Shortly, we can discuss why it is you don't trust your partner to inspect gear for you. But for now, let's address the fact that Paul didn't say what to do with the gear your partner handed you. Did he?"

"Well, uh, no, ma'am, I guess not. I guess I just figured this was another one of those 'trust' tests."

"Well, Byron. If it was one of those 'trust' tests, how do you think you did, I mean, based on results?"

"I trust my partner!" he said defensively.

"Do you?" Tallia pushed back. "Byron, if you trust your training partner, what is the concern around wearing gear someone else, your partner in your scenario, inspected?"

"Well, uh, I guess, I mean—"

"It's okay, Byron. Based upon the level of gasps in the room, you aren't the only person who still lacks trust in their partner relationship. Does anyone else have anything they'd like to add?"

Natazhia could hear the sound of Tristen's voice from the other side of the room, although, with the mountain between them, she couldn't see her.

"You set us up!" Tristen accused Tallia. "You wanted us to think we had to wear gear that our partner inspected."

"Maybe. That's a possible explanation, and yet doesn't that explanation bring even more awareness around the issue of trust? Can anyone else relate to feeling set up?"

Natazhia scanned the group and could see she wasn't the only one who felt set up and mistrusting. So, she continued to justify her feelings through self-talk.

Tallia confirmed Natazhia's thoughts when she spoke to the group again. "See, the fact that so many of you felt set up leaves us all in a bit of a pickle, doesn't it?"

Paul agreed with Tallia. "Yeah, we're all definitely in a bind. Let's see, y'all don't trust us when we give you rather simple instructions, and you are about to embark on a trek to the summit of Mount Everest, but you're stuck with us, whom you don't trust, as your guides. Yes, I'd say we're definitely in— What did you call it? A pickle?"

Natazhia felt herself drifting off into her thoughts again while the two bantered back and forth. *All right, I get it. I need to trust more. And I want to, but how? I mean, even when we seem to do everything right when it comes to this stuff, you all twist and turn it around, and suddenly good is bad, and bad is good. Up is down and down is up. I just don't know what will make you people okay with anything I do or anyone else does.*

"The instructions and the rules haven't changed since day one," Tallia said, reprimanding the group. "You agreed that you are responsible for your safety. You've always been responsible for your safety. You've been here for months and months. I would think that by this phase in your training, you would realize, first and foremost, your safety depends on your training partner's safety and vice versa. You and your partner are interdependent in this process. Furthermore, why would you continue to show up day after day and yet not have developed trust for your lead team? Or us?"

Tallia stopped talking and just looked around the room. Clearly, she was angry. The tension in the air was thick despite the cold and blowing air. Shivering, no one spoke for what felt like hours but was more likely five or ten minutes, while Tallia was pacing back and forth along the sides of the room between the chairs and the mountain. Finally, she broke the silence. "You know what, you're not ready." She called out, "Paul, shut it down."

The lights brightened, the mountain disappeared, and the room warmed up.

"We are unable to move forward as a team until we've completed Mount Everest, and it's unsafe for us to do so if we are not a team," Tallia said. "We are done here. You can stay in here and use this room if you'd like, or you can return to your living quarters. You all have some work to do. I'd start with your partner. Once the two of you have resolved the issues there, you need to come together as a team. If you figure that part out, well then, you can choose whether or not you can trust Paul and me and the rest of our team."

Tallia paused and looked around the outside of the room, all the while with a long, audible "ummm," indicating she was still thinking. Her eyes finally rested on Holly Love. "Holly? Why don't you stay and support them? If there's anyone here who they should trust by now, it would have to be you."

Several members of the group chuckled softly. Holly was bubbly, warm, and loving. She was like a mama bear to everyone. Tallia was probably right to choose her to work with the forty; everyone adored Holly.

Tallia and Paul promptly gathered up their belongings and as they started toward the doors, Tallia said, "Leads, the rest of you, come with us!" She continued mumbling to Paul as they left the room. While Natazhia couldn't hear their whispers, it was more than evident that Tallia was fuming.

When the doors closed behind the two, sighs of relief escaped the lips of many of the forty, and Natazhia felt a palpable release of tension. Almost everyone looked expectantly toward Holly, somewhat at a loss as to what to expect next.

"So now what?" Byron was the first to break the silence.

"I don't know about the rest of you, but I wasn't looking forward to climbing some mountain a bunch of people died trying to climb," Racyne said.

"You don't have a choice if you want to move on," Holly said matter-of-factly.

"What do you mean?"

"Yeah, what's that supposed to mean? Move on?"

Questions came from all around the room.

"Mount Everest is the final exercise, the final test," Holly explained. "It's the one that determines if you move on and remain part of the forty. It tests you mentally, physically, and spiritually. Only someone who passes the test remains." Holly paused to let her comments sink in. "But if you can't trust one another or your team, most of us, if not all of us, will fail."

"And what happens if we fail?" Natazhia asked.

"Well," Holly responded, "that's up to Zyra Kim. She could send you back up, above ground, or she might allow you to staff the kitchen or some other part of the overall operation. You'll have a chance to plead your case. On rare occasions, she's let some in the past try again with the replacements."

"What the hell do you mean, the past?" Tristen said, confronting her.

Holly laughed. "I'm sorry, Tristen, did you believe you were the first team to come down here to train?"

I knew it! I've always known something wasn't right. It is a setup. It's been a setup all along! "So, what's the point to all of this, then? What are we supposed to do, and how do we do it?" Natazhia asked. "What happens to those who don't get selected for a position?"

Holly said, "You go back up to what remains of the life you left behind, or you start a new one."

"So, either way then, this is over once we finish the test?" Racyne asked.

"Yes," Holly said, turning to Racyne and offering further explanation. "This phase of your training will be complete. Those who remain will advance into additional training phases depending on your assignment."

Natazhia spoke. "But what about being the chosen forty? Or is that all just for effect?"

Holly said, "There will be forty." She paused. "Eventually."

"What's that supposed to mean?" Tristen probed.

"Zyra has been searching for the forty for a very long time," Holly continued. "Unfortunately, not everyone who raises their hand possesses the courage or the character necessary to remain in the forty."

"Wait!" exclaimed Natazhia. "Did you just say we go back above ground if we aren't one of the forty?" She didn't give Holly time to respond before she continued questioning her. "But the bombings? What about the contamination? You seriously brought people down here, separated most of them from their families, and you're just going to send them back up to who knows what they are going to face because they didn't pass your test?"

"Whoa! First off, Natazhia, I'm not sending anyone anywhere, and it's not MY test to pass!"

"Okay, I'm sorry, Holly. I know you aren't in charge, but you are Zyra's representative, and you have the answers we need right now." Natazhia softened her tone. "Please, tell us what we need to know so we can move forward."

"I'll tell you everything I know and everything you need to know for all of you to choose what's next." Leading the way to the platform at the front of the room, Holly said, "Grab your chairs and bring them forward or find a spot on the floor, whatever's comfortable for you; we might be here a while."

Natazhia looked for Racyne on the other side of the room, and when she made eye contact, she raised her eyebrows and shrugged her shoulders, bending her arms with her palms up as if to ask, "What do you think?" Racyne responded with a nod and a shoulder shrug as if to say, "What have we got to lose?" Satisfied with her friend's response, she walked toward the front of the room and looked over her shoulder to ensure Dian was coming with her. Racyne, Dian, and Natazhia gathered at the front of the platform and waited until Tristen joined them before they sat down on the floor.

The conversation Natazhia was having with herself in her mind was almost deafening. *I've never felt this is right! Why the hell didn't I speak up? Why have I kept this from Ryker? Wait, does Ryker know about this? Surely Grayson Doyle knows. How could he keep this from me?*

Holly began to speak to those gathered, some sitting on chairs and others on the floor. "I'm glad that you all decided to stay. I know you have questions, just as I did when Zyra tested me. If you can hold on for a bit, I will share my experiences with you and give you some direction on how you might choose to move forward. After that, I will open the floor for questions, or if you are ready, I will give you the room to prepare for your next steps. Fair enough?"

Natazhia hesitated a moment and looked around the room to see the others nodding, then joined them and nodded her head in agreement.

Holly began to share her story. "I saw Zyra Kim speak at a Freedom Rally in Albuquerque, New Mexico. I was in awe of her and the vision she had; to create a world that works for everyone resonated deep in my heart. I waited in line at the front of the stage for hours until everyone else had left. Finally, I had my chance to talk to her. I begged her to hire me. I told her I would do anything she asked. I just wanted to be a part of her vision. I promised I would be the hungriest student she ever met. She handed me a book, and then she gave me a small device that had recordings from inspirational speakers dated between 2008 – 2025 before it was all wiped and abolished from the internet. And then she handed me a bracelet, much like the ones you have today. She told me that if I wanted to be a part of the resistance, I had to prove myself.

Like most of you, I never accepted the biometric currency chip (BCC). Had I, she would have required me to have it removed. As I'm sure you are aware, those who have it extracted risk infection and disease. And if you survive that, once the Liberation realizes that you've defected, they will never stop hunting for you, and the penalty for defection is torture and death. But I knew in my heart that even if I had a BCC, I would have done whatever she asked. Complying with the Liberation is not freedom, and I wanted freedom more than I valued my own life. She told me that once I accepted the bracelet, she would know when I was ready, and she would find me. Since I had refused the BCC, I was hesitant to wear a bracelet that seemed to do everything the BCC did, but the bracelet offered something the BCC did not. I would have the freedom to remove it without consequence, and I believed in her vision. Then she left. I slid the bracelet on and started back home about a half-day's walk away. I began listening to the recordings she gave me. Even after I returned home, I never stopped listening except to sleep and eat and read the book she gave me. I read the book over and over again. Everything about my attitude, character, and beliefs began to change. I already believed in freedom, but I didn't really understand what freedom was and how much we had given up, or how we had let it slip away. I knew that more people like me had to learn from what Zyra had.

"After about thirty days, I started to doubt she'd come back for me. I began to wonder what was wrong with me. I had done as she'd asked. I was a hungry student. And then I realized something about the bracelet that changed everything. I noticed there was a bead on it that sometimes was very dim and at other times was so bright that it kept me up at night. I realized that for a while, it had been very faint and I assumed it had stopped working. When I thought that Zyra would never find me again, I put the book away. I started listening less and less to the recordings of the speakers, and after a few days of not listening at all, the bracelet grew dimmer. I took it off, put it in a drawer, and gave up on ever being a part of the resistance and mentoring under Zyra Kim. Then there were rumblings that Zyra would be at a rally again. It was in St. George, Utah. I knew I had to be there. I knew it would take weeks, maybe even months, to get there and I would have to find a way to access the underground caves and tunnels since Colorado had become part of the Liberation and the fighting was intense along the Arizona border. I decided to leave right away. I knew I'd rather camp in Zion, where there were lots of places to hide for weeks, than miss an opportunity to plead with Zyra to take me with her. I took the bracelet out of the drawer where I hid it, took the audio device and book along with a journal and as much gear as I could pack. When I put the bracelet back on, the bead was brighter than I had ever experienced it, and for the first time in months, I felt hopeful. I set off on my trek, all the while listening to the audios I had abandoned."

Natazhia hung on every word. She could feel chills running down her spine and across her shoulders as Holly talked about her experience of the light with her bracelet.

I knew it! The colors of the stones are the key to something! But, what? Natazhia knew by her physical reaction that Holly was about to tell her what she needed to know. She reached in her bag and fumbled around for her journal, not wanting to miss anything Holly said. Once she felt it, she quickly pulled it out along with a pen from the bottom of her bag. Natazhia opened her journal across her lap and began taking notes as Holly continued her story.

"I started to take notice of the bead each day. I journaled every night by the fire and made sure I recorded everything—how many miles I'd traveled, what I ate, and how I felt. I began to see a correlation between how I felt and the brightness of the bead. I also noticed that my daily habits played a considerable role in how I felt each day. I made it my daily goal to make the bead as bright as possible every day. It was hard at first, especially on the days my feet hurt, or I had to travel through poor weather, or when I didn't get as far as I had planned. That was the worst. When I didn't meet my expectations, I hammered myself with criticism.

"By the time I arrived in St. George, I had learned how to keep the bracelet bright more often than it was dim. I had my days when it was hard; I'm not going to say I've mastered it even now or even completely understand it. I notice that the bracelet somehow measures the frequency of the energy I put out, and that's what powers the bead's glow. When I began to monitor it daily and adjust my state of being to increase its brightness, I discovered that I have the power to choose how I feel in any circumstance. I found that it had nothing to do with what I ate, how tired I was, or even how my physical body felt. I discovered I could choose how I felt regardless of the circumstances.

"You have the same tool available to you. Your bracelets are so much more advanced than the one Zyra gave me. Yours will tell you what frequency range you are operating at based on the stone's color on the inside of the bracelet."

After Holly finished speaking, Byron said, "Holly, that's a nice story, and sure, we've all noticed that these stupid bracelets monitor everything we do. But what does it have to do with passing the test and Mount Everest?

"Byron, do you recall what Zyra said to me when I first asked her to bring me with her?"

"Yeah," he said, "that she'd know when you were ready."

"Right," Holly said, nodding, "and as it turns out, my ability to manage my state at a high frequency was the test. She was able to monitor the bracelet's data the whole time I had it. When I finally arrived in St. George, Zyra allowed me to travel with them back down to Arizona after the rally. She made no promises, however I was there when Natazhia's husband chose the forty. I do believe the state of my energy is why he chose me."

Byron pressed Holly further. "Okay, but I still don't understand what that has to do with us sitting here right now."

"Team," Holly said, pleading with them convincingly, "this is *your* Mount Everest. Mine was to learn to manage my state on the journey from Albuquerque. I practice Mount Everest every single day."

They looked back at her, somewhat confused and trying to put all of the pieces together.

"So, we just have to make the stone turn a certain color?" Tristen asked.

Holly smiled. "Sort of; it's not quite that simple, though."

"Break it down for us, then," Racyne demanded.

"You will have the opportunity to face all of the elements of the real Mount Everest on the simulated one here in the arena. As you do, you will learn to manage your state regardless of the circumstances around you." Holly paused. "But, before you can even begin, you get to choose into trusting one another."

"What do you mean by *choose into?*" Dian said argumentatively. "Trust isn't a choice. I can't help it that someone else isn't trustworthy or that I'm not feeling it."

Holly pushed back. "How you feel, how you choose to respond to a circumstance, is *always* your choice, Dian. You don't expect me to believe that you cannot control your emotions, do you?"

"I guess not," Dian said, resigned. "So, how do we do it? What do we have to do to prove we trust one another?"

"You can't *do*, Dian," Holly said, "you get to *be*. Remember, the stone will always reveal the truth."

"Oh, for crying out loud," Byron said, exploding in frustration. "I don't know how these damn bracelets work, but even if I figured it out, there is no way *every single one of us* is going to trust all at the same time."

Holly smiled and gently responded. "Byron, you're probably right, and is there a way that you all can come together with a common goal, mission, or belief about this team that will create a bond that inspires trust?"

"I suppose."

"Terrific! I will leave you to it, then." Holly stood up and walked toward the doors as several of the group called out objections.

"Wait a minute!"

"You didn't tell us anything!"

"Help!"

She left the arena without looking back and the doors shut behind her.

10

CIRCLE OF TRUST

Everyone began speaking loudly after the door closed, the room erupting with voices full of questions and confusion, with no one listening to another.

Natazhia thought for a moment about everything Holly had shared with them. As she put the pieces together, chills traveled up her spine and across her shoulders again. *I wonder what that's all about.* She had been feeling the sensation several times that week, usually when she touched on a thought that seemed impossible yet somehow wasn't. Natazhia looked at her bracelet; the stone on the inside of her wrist glowed solid red. *What does that mean?* While she'd never seen it shine red before, Natazhia knew that it must be connected to God because she felt one with herself and the present moment. Her spine continuing to tingle, Natazhia stood up and yelled to get everyone's attention. "Hey, everyone, HEY! LISTEN UP!"

As the conversations subsided, the team impatiently gave her their attention.

"I think I understand what we need to do," Natazhia said, making eye contact with many in the group. "I've been watching the stone on my bracelet changing colors and for several weeks I've been journaling. I'm beginning to see a correlation between the colors and my feelings. There's a definite difference between the positive emotions and negative emotions, mostly in the vibrance of the colors."

Dismissively, Byron said, "We already heard Holly say the same thing. Get to the point."

"Right, the point—" Natazhia said. "I think we show that we are ready by all of us getting our stones to indicate positive states."

Tristen asked, "How are we supposed to do that? I can't control everyone else."

"No, Tristen, you can't," Natazhia said, nodding, "but Holly mentioned goals or purpose or something along that line. I think if we come up with a phrase that when we say it or even feel it, we immediately trigger positive emotions. If we can all agree on the same word or phrase, we can use it to remind one another to check in with ourselves and shift our state if we are in a negative one."

"Natazhia?" Racyne asked, "How do we shift our state?"

"Good question, Racyne, I'm not entirely sure I know the answer, but changing my daily thoughts and habits, along with being more aware of my emotions, has made it easier for me to recognize and change them."

"But, how do common words or a phrase help?"

"Honestly, I don't know for sure that they will. I remember my mother talking about watching sports competition when she was a child. She said they always had a mascot and a chant of some kind that brought them together. I think that's what Holly was suggesting."

"I think I'm tracking with you now," Byron said, smiling. "So, you think if we pick something we all believe in, we can use that to trigger us to come together?"

"YES!" She responded confidently, then continued with much less conviction, "maybe; it's worth a try, anyway."

"I think you're onto something, Natazhia," Byron said. "What phrase do you suggest we use?"

"Byron, I think we all still need to agree on that. I certainly don't have anything in mind," Natazhia replied, looking around the room for the board she had seen Tallia 'write on' by speaking into her bracelet. Locating the board, she pointed toward it and said, "Somebody, please bring the board over here." She continued to scan the room until her eyes landed on Tristen. "Hey Tristen, you don't miss anything, and you're up on technology, so, can you figure out how to make stuff show up on the board while I come up with a plan?" Natazhia walked over toward the platform where Holly had sat earlier. Now it was her turn to lead the group. "Let's all throw around some ideas and see what sticks."

They spent hours discussing whether they should create a mission statement or just list several qualities they wanted the team to represent. At times they argued and became frustrated. Natazhia reminded everyone to 'check in' with themselves by monitoring the stone inside their bracelets. Finally, at 7:30 pm, after spending the entire day in the arena, Natazhia looked at the time, satisfied that at last they had landed on something.

"Byron, would you like to do the honor and read it?"

"Um, yeah, okay. We, The Forty, shall lead the New World as Trustworthy, Compassionate, and Courageous citizens."

"Okay, sounds good! How about we all say it together?"

Together and in unison, everyone spoke with strong voices. "WE, THE FORTY, SHALL LEAD THE NEW WORLD AS TRUSTWORTHY, COMPASSIONATE, AND COURAGEOUS CITIZENS!"

"Yes!" Natazhia said, rubbing her arms, still feeling goosebumps from chanting their team statement in one voice. "Can you all feel that?" As she looked around the room, everyone was nodding. "Quick, look at your stone!" She was curious to see if they were all the same color.

After looking for themselves, everyone raised their arms, turning their wrists toward her so she could see the color of their stones.

While Natazhia could see a variety of colors, none were the washed-out pale shades that she had seen when she was experiencing negative emotions.

“That’s the answer!” Natazhia said excitedly. “Any time we notice ourselves or anyone else experiencing a negative emotion, that’s when we say our statement to shift our team into a positive state. By all proclaiming we are trustworthy, then trust exists!”

Dian spoke up. “Not to be a buzz killer, but does this mean we can go eat now?”

Everyone began to nod, and Natazhia laughed. “Yes, I think it’s safe for us to go eat. When I get back to the living quarters, I’ll visit Holly and let her know we are ready for Mount Everest tomorrow.”

When Natazhia entered the arena the following day with Dian by her side, a cold blast of air greeted them. The mountain had reappeared in the center of the room. They walked along the outside of the room and found chairs labeled with their names. The previous night, the team had formed a new bond. Everyone was smiling, confident and eager to begin their day. Regardless of what each team member wanted after they passed the test, they were confident of one thing; they were a team now, and the team would pass the test.

“Congratulations!” Tallia opened the session by celebrating their victory. “You came together as a team, and it appears you are ready to face your final test.” Smiling broadly, she nodded to Paul at her side.

“You may recall when we first gathered in this arena, we mentioned that a select few of you have the opportunity to be a part of the leadership team.” Paul paused a moment to allow the group to focus their thoughts. “You will ascend the mountain in squads of four to five, which means we need five Squad Leaders. We’ve been evaluating your growth and your performance since the moment you entered the cave. And, should you choose to accept the role, Byron Shields, Dian Lister, Racyne Brenner, Tristen Marks, and Natazhia Flynn, we welcome you to consider being Squad Leaders.”

Natazhia and her friends searched the room for one another, attempting to make eye contact. She was surprised that all of the leaders Paul selected were her closest friends except for Byron. *You are the sum of the five people you hang out with.* Natazhia heard the words her mother often repeated throughout her childhood echoing in her thoughts. *Well, how the heck does Byron fit into this group then? He's the last person I want to be around!* She wasn't sure she wanted to take on the responsibility of Squad Leader, and yet Natazhia thought it could be the way to get more of her questions answered. Making eye contact with Racyne, Natazhia gave the slightest nod in her friend's direction.

"Are you going to leave us in suspense?" Tallia asked no one in particular. "This is an honor to be celebrated. Get on up here if you accept the position."

The five of them slowly stood up and walked toward the edge of the mountain where Tallia and Paul stood. When they all reached the front, Tallia and Paul in turn shook each of their hands and offered congratulations. Then Paul announced, "World Changers, allow me to introduce you to your Squad Leaders!"

The remaining forty clapped, and Natazhia felt curious to know how many were clapping because they were genuinely excited for the new leadership team and how many felt obligated to clap.

"Go ahead and sit down, team," Tallia said. "We've got a lot left to do to prepare for Everest. I need the five of you to stay behind when we release the rest of the team."

Natazhia, her closest friends, and Byron walked back to their seats, and Tallia and Paul addressed the team.

"Again, congratulations," Tallia said, "for doing some incredible work yesterday. You may not be fully aware of all that you accomplished. With the statement, WE, THE FORTY, SHALL LEAD THE NEW WORLD AS TRUSTWORTHY, COMPASSIONATE, AND COURAGEOUS CITIZENS! you have established the foundation and context for your vision of the New World. Your statement will bring us together as a team, and it will also serve as our identity in much the same way as the words of the Declaration of Independence once served our founding fathers and many generations to follow. I would encourage each of you to consider writing personal statements that support you as your leadership journey continues."

As Natazhia listened to Tallia, she considered some of the qualities in the statement that most resonated for her. She felt that courage was a struggle for her. More than anything, though, she wanted to be a courageous leader. While others saw her as bold, she felt like an imposter. *The truth is, I'm the opposite of courageous; I'm scared of almost everything. What if I fail? Ryker is courageous; Serenity is courageous. My boys are some of the bravest people I know. I'm here because my kids inspire me to fight for them.* Natazhia fought for her children because she loved them and was accountable to them, not because she had courage. Still, she felt like she didn't have a choice but to be courageous. She knew better, of course. The reality was that despite how she felt, she could choose to be courageous even when she didn't feel that way. But the truth was that Natazhia desperately wanted to retreat to their home and live the life they'd been living long before they listened to Zyra Kim at the trading post. She didn't want to disappoint her husband or friends. *Am I qualified to be a squad leader?*

The sound of Paul's voice returned her attention to the present. "Okay, mates! Let's give it another go, whaddya say?" He paused to ensure he had everyone's attention. "Remove the packs from below your seats and ensure the pack has your name on it."

Natazhia and the others reached under their chairs and checked the tags on their packs to ensure they had their own.

"Once you've confirmed you have the correct pack, take a few moments to inspect your gear. Ensure there are no holes, tears, or loose threads in the outerwear. Scrutinize your ropes for any sign of weakness. Remove the packing list from the front pocket and use it to inventory the items in your pack. Once you are confident your pack is safe and ready, you may ask your partner to double-check it for you, if you choose."

The forty spent the next hour chatting among themselves as they inventoried their packs and then inventoried their partner's packs.

When Paul and Tallia were satisfied the team was complete, Tallia called out over the noise. "You may all leave the arena. I don't want to see you for the next four and a half days. I think you deserve some time off."

Her announcement sparked even more noise as the forty cheered.

Tallia wasn't finished and increased her volume. "Except for the squad leaders," she called out. "You will be training with Holly, Professor, Loren, Jerome, and me."

Natazhia's heart sank. Even if only for a few seconds, the idea of four and a half days of relaxation and family time excited her. She was already doubting the decision she'd made to accept the squad leader position. After the others left the room, she joined Racyne, Tristen, Dian, and Byron at the front of the room to meet with Paul, Tallia, and the others. While the leads continued talking among themselves, Natazhia felt awkward eavesdropping on their conversation, and sensed tension in the air. Jerome and Professor spoke to one another in hushed whispers, carefully looking around to see if anyone might hear. Holly and Loren stood by, listening intently and looking out the corners of their eyes as if on high alert.

The uneasiness Natazhia had felt on other occasions came rushing back. Still hopeful that she'd get to the bottom of whatever was happening behind the scenes that contributed to her mistrust, she turned her wrist to check in with her emotions on the bracelet stone. It was pale lime green. Through her journaling, Natazhia was almost sure that color came up when she felt anxious or afraid, and it came up often. *See, I'm not at all courageous; even this stupid bracelet can see that. I don't know what they were thinking by choosing me. I should have just said no. I wonder if it's too late for them to find someone else.* Her thoughts racing, Natazhia focused on the stone and watched as the color lightened even more. Clearly self-talk adversely affected her. *Shut up!* Natazhia adjusted the quality of her thinking. *And there's no way you could have married a brave man or raised those incredible kids without some amount of courage. You've got this.* As she shifted her thoughts, the stone color also changed, first back to the lime green, then it began to turn bluer. Satisfied that she was gaining some control over her emotions, Natazhia's attention tuned into other conversations going on in the room.

A moment later, when Professor caught her gaze and motioned to the others to stop their conversation, there was an awkward moment of silence. Then he walked over to Tallia and Paul and interrupted their conversation by leaning in to whisper something to Tallia. Natazhia watched as a look of surprise, then anger swept across Tallia's face.

Tallia put on a huge, ingenuine smile, and called out to everyone in the room. "All right, squad leaders, gather around; let's get started!"

Racyne looked at Natazhia with raised eyebrows, and Natazhia responded with a questioning look. Racyne moved closer and whispered to her friend. "They seem secretive like something is going on. I don't like it."

Natazhia sighed with relief. "I thought I was just paranoid. Yeah, I think something's up too."

The two waited for Dian and Tristen to join them, still unsure about Byron. The women were protective of Natazhia, and Byron had said his share of hateful things about her. They were all wary of the impact of his presence on the team dynamics.

As they approached the holographic mountain, Tallia raised her bracelet toward her mouth and offered a command of some sort. Mount Everest again disappeared, and the temperature in the room warmed instantly.

"Sit down, and let's go over what the next couple of days are going to look like," Tallia said as they all pulled chairs together in a small circle. "You will spend the majority of your time here, except for short dinner breaks and a brief period of shut-eye during each 24-hour segment."

Paul spoke next. "You must hydrate and choose good nutrition during your breaks. The final test will be physically and mentally demanding, especially for you. You are responsible for yourselves and one another; each of you will also have a team looking to you for leadership, courage, and protection."

Natazhia was nervous, and doubt crept into her thoughts again; *there it is again—courage, but I'm not brave. How am I supposed to keep the others safe?* She recognized the change in her energy almost immediately and corrected herself. *I am a courageous woman, and I'm not going to listen to your negativity. I've got this. Listen to the instructions.* Natazhia reached for her messenger bag she'd slung over the chair earlier and fumbled around for her pen and notebook again. *I need to shut off my brain and focus.* She hoped taking notes would keep her mind from wandering into those dark places.

They spent the remainder of the day partnered with the lead team members while Paul and Tallia drifted from one pair to the next. Allen Rice became Natazhia's training partner mentor. As they tucked themselves off in one of the corners, Professor put her nervousness at ease almost immediately.

"I'm so excited they assigned you to me," Professor said. "I've been very impressed with how you've handled yourself from the start. Especially the way you've stood up for yourself and your family."

His affirmation made Natazhia feel much better about her role on the team. "Thank you, and I didn't think anyone noticed or cared."

"Oh, it's been noticed." He laughed. "At least I've noticed; I'm sure others have too. Why do you think you're part of the team?"

"I don't know; I figured it had more to do with Ryker working so closely with Grayson Doyle and Zyra Kim."

After a good bit of small talk, Allen began asking Natazhia questions about her childhood and how she felt growing up. At first, she thought he might genuinely be interested, but as the day wore on, and he kept pushing her to connect with feelings about different circumstances in her life, it turned into therapy. Often crying, she felt as though she was on an emotional roller coaster.

When the team broke for meals, she was disappointed to learn that she would spend that time with Allen instead of her friends. She desperately wanted to check in with them to compare notes. The brighter lighting in the dining hall allowed Natazhia to at least connect visually with the women. Judging by Tristen's puffy red eyes, she assumed they were going through the same emotional process with their lead mentors. The break was less than thirty minutes long, however, it was a welcome break from the heavy questions while Professor was more focused on the meal in front of him.

When they returned to the arena, Tallia joined Natazhia and Allen. Tallia's line of questioning made Professor appear friendly. Natazhia felt as though Tallia disapproved of her, because it didn't matter how Natazhia answered, Tallia wanted more. She made her dig deeper and even made her close her eyes, seemingly in an attempt to hypnotize her. Natazhia grew more and more uncomfortable.

Tallia must have noticed because, at one point, she attempted to soothe her. "Natazhia, I know this is hard. It's all part of the process. I'm here because I genuinely care about you and your family. I care about all of humanity spread out across the planet. You are in a safe space, and I'm doing this for you."

Natazhia recalled her team's statement and knew she had to let her guard down. So, she did. She opened herself up to trusting the process and allowed Paul, Tallia, and Professor to coach her. She opened herself up and became coachable. She accepted their feedback as truth, no matter how much it hurt, and resolved to change.

The process went on for several days. Natazhia wasn't sure she even knew who she was anymore. She felt as though they were breaking and then re-programming her. On one level, she felt more confident, more aware, and believed the process made her a better person. On the other hand, however, she yearned for the comfort of remaining blind to her flaws. There was never a time since they'd entered the mine shaft that Natazhia longed for Racyne and Tristen's companionship more. She wondered if they felt the same and if they were okay.

After what seemed like an eternity, though according to the date and time on Natazhia's bracelet, it was only three and a half days later, Tallia called them all back together as one group, and then it started all over again. Only this time, the others watched. Now it was even more difficult for Natazhia to respond, wondering what the others thought of her, and yet she felt compelled to answer honestly and vulnerably. She had surrendered to their process. Even so, her heart ached as she watched her friends open up and share things with the group that they had never shared with her. She felt like a bad friend for not knowing, and she was angry with Tallia for forcing them to share such painful memories. She also felt confused. *What does all of this have to do with training us to be squad leaders?* Throughout the entire ordeal, Natazhia witnessed the leads and Paul and Tallia huddling together in pairs or small groups, whispering while cautiously looking around to ensure no one could hear their words.

After an emotional morning, Paul announced that it was time to break for lunch. He stood up and loudly clapped his hands together, then began wringing them as though he were nervous. "All righty, mates. It's time. We have every bit of confidence that you are prepared to lead and coach your teams. You may go and enjoy lunch with whomever you please. After lunch, take three and a half days of R & R to prepare for the journey on the mountain. Early tomorrow morning, we will give the remaining forty their instructions for the trip to Base Camp, where they will acclimate to the conditions and terrain. Zyra Kim and Grayson Doyle will expeditiously drop you off at the rendezvous point at the appropriate time."

"Wait!" Byron said. "Are you saying we are not going to be with the rest of the team?" He paused. "Or with the rest of the leadership team?"

Tallia stepped in and answered for Paul. "Byron, that's not at all what Paul said," she said, trying to reassure him. "The lead team will also participate in R & R over the next few days, and they will travel with you to Base Camp. Paul and I will accompany the others and be waiting when you arrive."

Natazhia looked at Racyne, who was still sitting next to her. If the confused look on her friend's face was any indication, she was as concerned about the twist of events as Byron seemed to be. Natazhia agreed; something wasn't right.

Tallia seemed to want to avoid any further questions and leaned over, grabbed her bag, threw it over her shoulder, then stood up and looked at Paul. He gave the nod, and the two walked toward the door, as Paul called over his shoulder, "See ya at camp!"

11

THE BETRAYAL

The intensely emotional ride they had individually and all experienced dropped them into silence together—Natazhia and her friends stared at one another. Byron stood a few steps away, looking back and forth between the lead team and the four women he now worked alongside as a squad leader. He didn't seem sure of where he fit.

"It's all right, Byron," Natazhia said. "I'm willing to let the past go by the wayside."

"I apologize, Natazhia; I'm really sorry. I should never have treated you the way I did,"

"Friends?" she asked, holding out her hand.

"Friends," Byron said and shook her outstretched hand.

"I don't know—" Tristen added playfully.

Following her lead, Racyne crossed her arms and said, "It might take a lot more than an apology to convince us."

Byron looked at the two of them, not quite sure if they were serious. When the women all burst into laughter, a smile spread across his face. He stretched out his arms and said, "Bring it in for a group hug, ladies!"

Afterward, Byron looked over at the group of lead trainers gathered on the far side of the room, and asked them, "What's all the secretiveness about, anyway? I mean, why aren't we all leaving as a team?"

The lead team looked at one another as though they weren't sure how to answer Byron's questions. Finally, Jerome spoke up. "You'll find there are a lot of things you aren't privy to as squad leaders. Nothing happens by accident here; you'll know soon enough."

In silence, Byron and the four women exchanged glances again. Each looked more confused by Jerome's response than they felt before he answered, but the lead team didn't stick around long enough for them to ask additional questions.

"Hey, will you make sure the lights are out when you leave?" Professor said as they walked out the door. "See you in a few days."

"Uh, yeah, okay, Professor," Byron answered.

The five of them stood there in silence for a moment, unsure of what to say. Finally, Dian broke the silence. "Hey, look, you guys. I'm not trying to be suspicious or anything, but something isn't right."

"I agree," Racyne said as the others nodded their heads.

"I don't know about y'all, but I'm starving," Tristen said. "I agree with you both, so how 'bout we take this conversation to the dining hall?"

"Agreed," said Byron.

They gathered their packs and the belongings they'd brought to class and headed out.

"Do you all mind if we stop by the living quarters beforehand to unload some of this stuff?" Natazhia asked.

"I second that," Racyne said.

The five of them walked in silence, each lost in their thoughts, trying to make sense of Paul and Tallia's behavior and Jerome's explanation.

When the five squad leaders arrived at the living quarters, they could hear the lead team talking and laughing loudly in the kitchen. When Byron and the four women turned the corner and appeared, the lead team's laughter changed to hushed whispers; they picked up their drinks from the table where they'd been sitting and quickly left the room. The squad leaders looked at one another. No one had to speak; they agreed something didn't add up. They split up and headed off to their rooms, and as they did, Racyne asked rhetorically, "Meet back here in five?"

Natazhia was relieved to find her family was still out. After being gone almost around the clock the last several days, she wasn't sure she'd want to leave if they were there. She tossed her bags on the floor by the door and went down the hall to the kids' bathroom to see clear evidence that she hadn't been there much; the kids had thrown towels all over the place, and it was obvious at least one of the twins didn't lift the seat. Frustrated, she headed down the hall to her bathroom instead. After splashing water on her face and running a brush through her hair, she rushed back out to meet her friends for dinner.

She was the first one to make it back to the dayroom, so she plopped herself down on one of the couches. *They better hurry up; if they take too long, I'll be asleep, and there won't be anyone getting me off this couch.* She stretched and closed her eyes, hoping for a minute or two of rest.

Seconds later, she heard Racyne, Tristen, and Dian talking as they came down the hall from their dorms, and then Byron called. "Y'all ready?"

With a groan, Natazhia sat up on the sofa and slowly stood up. "Let's go; I don't know how much longer I'm going to last."

The dining hall was empty when they arrived except for Paul and Tallia, seated at a corner table with their dinner finished, plates pushed to the side. They both leaned over the table and appeared to be drawing on something. Natazhia nudged Racyne with her elbow and nodded her head in their direction. The five of them continued to walk toward the food line, hoping their presence would go unnoticed by the two.

Natazhia breathed in the aroma of the fresh-baked bread and savory garlic. The cooks had prepared chicken breasts with pesto sauce and garlic mashed potatoes. Natazhia hoped that one day she would be privy to how the food made its way underground to their compound. Nonetheless, Natazhia was grateful for a hot meal after a week of grabbing snacks from their kitchen each night since the dining hall had been closed when they left the arena.

After they filled their plates, and the five returned to the main dining room, Paul and Tallia had disappeared.

"Let's grab that one," Byron said, pointing to the table Paul and Tallia had occupied a few minutes earlier.

Curious, Natazhia shrugged her shoulders and said, "Okay," then looked back at the other women and nodded her head in the direction of the table.

When they sat down, Racyne said, "Why this table, Byron?"

"Look, we all know they are up to something and they don't want anyone finding out about it, right?" Byron said as he made eye contact with each of them.

The women immediately nodded as they started eating their meals, encouraging him to continue.

"Okay, then. I'm pretty sure they know where to discuss their plans without surveillance cameras hearing what they are saying. And, judging by the fact they were also writing on something, I'm going to guess this table is also out of view of the cameras. We don't need them seeing or hearing that we are suspicious, even if it turns out there's no reason for us to be."

Dian was the first to speak. "Woah, Byron. I guess it's a good thing they put you on squad after all. I know I wouldn't have thought of those things." Looking at the others, she said, "Would any of you have put that together?"

Racyne, Tristen, and Natazhia each shook their heads in response to Dian, their mouths too full to respond.

"So, Byron," Racyne said after wiping her mouth with her napkin, "what do you think is going on, then?"

"I don't know, but I've been watching Paul and Tallia and some of the lead trainers for a while now, and I'm convinced they are not on the same team we are."

"Wait, what?" Natazhia asked in a surprised whisper. "You, too? I've just felt like something was like a setup of some sort, not necessarily that they're not on the same team as us."

"Natazhia!" Racyne said urgently, also in a low voice, "why am I just now hearing this? Don't you trust me? Wait! Did the rest of you know?"

Dian and Tristen both shook their heads.

"It's not that I don't trust *you*; it's *me* I don't trust," Natazhia said, reassuring them. "Ryker says I'm paranoid. I thought I was just making stuff up in my head."

Byron said, "You are most definitely not being paranoid. I think they are planning a coup."

"No way. Really? What makes you think that, Byron?" Tristen asked.

"I think Paul and Tallia want what we want, except I think they want to be the ones to make it happen instead of Zyra. I think they want control of the compound, and they want Zyra out of the way."

"What on earth makes you think that?" Natazhia asked.

"Why do you think they chose all of you as squad leaders? Doesn't it seem odd that you and Dian are partners and Racyne and Tristen are your closest friends? Why would they pick all four of you?"

"I don't know," she said defensively. "I guess it was 'cause they saw something in us. I mean, we all, including you, were the ones who led the team through their trust test."

"True," Byron said, nodding his head, "but you are married to Ryker, who is the right-hand man to Zyra's second-in-command. Paul and Tallia know that there's no way you would ever choose allegiance to them over your husband. So, I'm guessing they believe that your closest friends would remain loyal you. They must have chosen the four of you to distract everyone from seeing the truth and to keep a closer eye on you."

Natazhia said only half-jokingly, "I suppose that makes some sense, but then how does that explain you being here with us, Byron? Let's face it; there was never any loyalty between us."

Byron chuckled. "No, you're right, no love lost there. They know I suspect them, and the fact that they've separated the five of us from the rest of the group tells me I'm more right about them than I am wrong. But, Natazhia, tell me—"

Racyne interrupted Byron. "Wait, I don't understand. How do they know you suspect them?"

"Loren told them," Byron said. "I noticed Paul and Tallia behaving oddly a while back, and I asked him."

"Why the hell would you go ask one of their favorites? That's kinda dumb if you ask me!" Tristen blurted out.

"Loren and I were business partners before this all started," he said. "We had a tent at the trading post together, and we've been friends for over ten years. I thought I could trust him."

Tristen felt terrible about calling Byron dumb. "Dude, man. Hey, I'm sorry, I didn't know; it sucks."

"Yeah," Byron said, "it does. Natazhia, we need to compare notes. Tell me what you've seen, and I can tell you what I've seen, then we can figure out what to do from there."

As the five of them sat at the table, in between bites, Natazhia shared the numerous occasions when she observed Paul and Tallia or the lead trainers being secretive or appearing to hide something. She even shared her experience with the clothier the day they'd arrived at the trading post and how, although she couldn't give a reason, her intuition told her that he had something to do with what was going on.

"Does your husband know all of this?" Byron asked.

"Well, I did mention my misgivings about the clothier at the trading post, but since then, I haven't mentioned my suspicions about Paul and Tallia or what's going on here. Like I told you, he would think I'm paranoid. I've been watching them closely and hoping to gather proof," Natazhia said as she pulled apart the warm bread, "but honestly, after all the work we did with them this week and getting to know Allen and Holly, I don't think they are involved. I mean, perhaps they know something, just like we do, but I don't think they'd take part in a coup. Do you?"

"Yeah, no way Holly is part of something like that," Dian said, agreeing with her. "She's my lead partner, and she worships Zyra. She wouldn't knowingly hurt her."

Byron pushed back. "But you've seen them all together. I'm telling you; Loren was my best friend for over ten years, and he still turned on me. They are all involved; there's no way you will convince me otherwise."

"Maybe it's not as big of a deal as we're making it," Tristen said. "I mean, yes, they're acting suspiciously, and they're making plans of some kind. But that doesn't mean they have to be planning a coup. They could be planning something with Zyra."

"I guess it's possible," Byron sighed as he pushed his empty plate toward the center of the table, "but if that's the case, why wouldn't they have let us in on the secret now that we are squad leaders?"

"Good point, Byron," Natazhia said. "I say we ask them. Now that we are leaders, they should confide in us. If they don't, we should tell Zyra what we've seen."

"So, who's asking them?" Racyne said.

"I'll ask Holly," said Dian.

"I'll see if Professor will tell me anything," Natazhia said, "and I'll also talk to Ryker. If Zyra does know what's going on, I'm sure he and Grayson are in the loop."

"Okay, but let's agree that's it; we don't discuss this with anyone else," Byron said, warningly, looking at each of them intently. "We have to keep it between us until we know for sure."

The others nodded in agreement.

"And we wait until after Paul and Tallia leave with the others tomorrow morning," Byron added.

"Yep," said Tristen nodding, "I agree, don't give them any hint that we're on to them."

"All right, it's a plan," Natazhia said as she stood up. "Let's talk tomorrow. I'm going to get some rest, hug my children, and find out what Ryker knows."

Everyone else stood up, and after dropping off their empty plates and utensils in the kitchen, they headed back to the living quarters. Natazhia felt better about sharing her concerns with Ryker now that she knew she wasn't alone in her suspicions. She was relieved to have the others onside with her to get to the bottom of whatever it was Paul and Tallia were hiding. When they arrived at the living quarters, they stopped in the dayroom to say good night, taking turns to hug each other before heading to their rooms.

Natazhia took a deep breath before opening the door to her family's quarters. Ryker hated problems, so she hated bringing them to his attention. As grateful as she was that she no longer had to keep her concerns a secret, she wanted to spend her time off enjoying her family. She had learned if the timing was wrong, enjoyment was not possible because problems negatively impacted his mood and disposition. When she opened the door, the boys ran toward her, and she braced herself so they wouldn't throw her off balance.

"Hey guys, did you miss me?" she asked as they had a group hug.

Jacob and Blaise began talking to her excitedly over one another so that it was impossible to make out what either said. Natazhia laughed as they followed her to Serenity's room. She knocked on her daughter's closed bedroom door, then opened it and poked her head in the doorway.

"Hey, Ren," she said softly, "I missed you."

"Mom!" Serenity exclaimed as she jumped off the bed where she had been reading a book. The book fell to the floor, and Serenity gave her mom a long hug. "I'm glad you're home."

"Me too. Where's your dad?"

"He's still not home. I think something may be going on. He seems kinda stressed out."

"Did you kids get a chance to eat?"

"Yeah, Mom. I made pizzas in the galley. The boys didn't want to go to the dining hall."

"I guess that means we get to hang out for a bit, then." Arms around each other, mother and daughter strolled back to the living room and piled on the couch with the twins. "What do you kids want to do?"

"Can we just watch some of the old home movies and pictures that you keep on that old phone of yours, Mom?"

"Yeah, please, Mom!" Jacob pleaded. "I miss home."

"That sounds like a great way to spend the evening," Natazhia said, happily agreeing with her children. "I miss home, too."

Natazhia found the old phone, another treasure Ryker had brought her when he returned with the kids. They spent the next hour looking at pictures and short video clips from their old life. Natazhia yearned to be back at their home where she didn't have to deal with the responsibility of worrying about leading anyone except her children. Exhausted, she fell asleep on the couch with the kids cuddled on both sides of her.

It was almost morning before Ryker came in. "What is going on here?" He stopped inside the door and began laughing when he saw them all piled on the couch.

Natazhia opened her eyes and smiled. "You're home."

The children kept sleeping while Natazhia gently moved them so she could get up and greet her husband. She walked to the entryway where he stood, emptying his pockets of tools and other items and placing them on the side table. She hugged him and kissed his neck. "Is everything okay?"

"I'm sure it will be," he said. "There's just a lot we are dealing with internally right now."

"Does it have anything to do with Paul and Tallia?"

Ryker appeared surprised by her question. "What do you know about—" then stopped himself and said, "I mean, why do you ask that?"

Seeing her opening, Natazhia said, "I knew it! It does have something to do with them!"

"What are you— Wait, I didn't say anything about it having to do with them. Why do you think that, though?" Her husband fumbled with his words as he tried to recover from sharing too much.

"You have said enough. Look, we know they're up to something. I was planning to talk to you about it when you got home." Smiling with relief, she shared with him what she and the others had discussed the day before, including her suspicions, and Byron's tip about the cameras.

"Why didn't you say something sooner?"

"You always accuse me of being paranoid."

"I guess I do; I'm sorry. You're very intuitive, and I guess I just haven't paid attention in the past." Taking her in his arms, he said, "Look, I can't give you details, but I can tell you Zyra and Grayson already know everything and they are handling it. They are committed to carrying out our mission with excellence. You are right to be careful who you trust. I can't tell you what to do, but I would keep further discussion between only the five of you."

Pouting playfully, Natazhia looked up at her husband. "I guess this means we aren't getting much in the way of rest and relaxation over the next few days, are we?"

"No, unfortunately not." Ryker sighed. "But the kids are still asleep, and I'm beat. What do you say we take a short nap before they wake up, then we can all have breakfast? After that, I'll go brief Zyra and Grayson on what you've all seen and heard."

Natazhia let out a disappointed sigh, "Okay," she said, smiling. "A short nap is better than nothing." She was careful not to put too much pressure on her husband, knowing how hard he was on himself. Natazhia followed her husband to their bedroom, where they collapsed, both of them physically, mentally, and emotionally exhausted.

The kids slept for several more hours before their parents were waking them up in time to enjoy a big breakfast. They were all happy that the dining hall had been opened for breakfast during the scheduled R & R. Natazhia and Ryker walked the boys to the children's center, and Serenity went to the teen center since they also had time off from school. As the door to the children's center closed behind the boys, Ryker kissed Natazhia on her forehead, and said, "I gotta go, babe; it's all going to work out. I promise. Just remember what I said. Be careful who you trust. I love you."

"I love you too," she replied as she put her hands on each side of his face and kissed his lips. "You be careful, too. When will I see you again?"

Ryker sighed heavily. "I think it's going to be a long day for both of us. I'm not going to make any promises, but I will try to meet you and the kids for dinner. Let's say around 6:30? Will that work?"

"We will be there. I love you."

As she walked toward the living quarters, she thought to herself, *Okay, now it's time to see what Professor will tell me.* Her heart began beating a little harder and a lump formed in her throat. After spending time with him the prior week, she genuinely liked Professor and hoped he wasn't part of anything that would put a wedge between them.

As she entered the dayroom at the living quarters, she was pleased to find Professor by himself in one of the reading chairs. He had a crossword puzzle in front of him and a pencil and a pair of reading glasses barely hanging on to the bridge of his nose.

"Hey Professor, do you have a minute?"

Startled, he looked up to see who had disturbed him, and the corners of his scowl softened, spreading into a warm smile. "Sure, Natazhia. What can I do for you?"

Nervously, she began with small talk. "What are you working on there, Allen?"

"Oh, just a crossword puzzle; it helps me keep my mind sharp. But I know you didn't come to talk to an old man about crossword puzzles. What's on your mind, dear?"

"Honestly, Professor, I don't know where to start."

"Well, how about at the beginning?" He smiled. "That always seems like a good place to start."

"Okay, then, well, the thing is over the last few months, one of the other squad leaders and I noticed a lot of secretive behavior between Paul and Tallia, and it seems like we see it more and more often."

Professor listened intently, not indicating what he might be thinking. "I see, and why exactly are you telling me? Shouldn't you ask them about their behavior? Seems to me this may be gossip."

Flustered by his response, Natazhia felt her face heat up as she flushed with embarrassment that he would accuse her of gossip. "No, sir, that's not at all what I meant. It's just we've noticed that you and the other lead trainers are also having conversations with them and with each other. It's always awkward when one of us notices, you know, like you don't want us to hear you, or it's a secret. We are just concerned that we may not know everything we should to, um, you know, um, get our teams through the final test."

He laughed, although there was a tension between them that wasn't usually there, and the laugh seemed forced. Natazhia felt the hairs stand up on the back of her neck. She knew he was about to lie to her.

"Natazhia, dear girl," he said condescendingly, "you can rest assured that you and the other squad leaders know all that you need to know. You should take this time and rest rather than worry about things that don't involve you and your little friends."

Her face grew hotter as he showed himself to be less the man than she believed. "But, Prof—" she said, trying to object.

"No, young lady, there are no buts, except to butt out of things that are none of your business," he said, interrupting her before she had a chance to finish. "I'm sure you have a lot of more productive things you can be doing right now, and I am also on R & R, so if you will excuse me, I'm going to get back to my crossword puzzles." He opened his book and looked down again, shutting her out even though she was still sitting in the chair next to him.

It took a few seconds to regain her composure before standing up; she took a deep breath, then nodded curtly and said, "Thank you for your time today, Professor." Then she walked away.

A moment later, when Natazhia opened the door of her living quarters, she looked back at Allen to ensure he wasn't watching her. Satisfied, she shoved the door so it would swing all the way open, and then, with a glance over her shoulder, she rushed toward Racyne's room before the door slammed shut. When she arrived at Racyne's door, she lightly tapped on it—loud enough to get her friend's attention and quiet enough so that Professor wouldn't hear the sound echoing down the hallway.

A few seconds later, although it felt like minutes to Natazhia, Racyne cracked open the door.

"Quick, let me in," Natazhia whispered, pushing past the door into her friend's room.

"What is going on, Natazhia?"

"I, uh, um. I just got done talking to Professor."

"And?"

"He basically told me to butt out, and that it was none of our business."

"Oh man, I really hoped they weren't part of whatever Paul and Tallia are up to. Or wait, are we sure they are up to anything? I mean maybe that's why he said that."

Natazhia leaned against the wall in her friend's entryway and shook her head. "Yes, something is going on. Ryker was with Grayson and Zyra all night. He didn't give me any details, but he said whatever it is, Zyra is aware and it will be handled. He also said not to talk to anyone else not already involved."

"So, what do we do now?"

"I don't know, I guess we wait and see if Holly really is loyal to Zyra and shares anything with Dian."

"And if she doesn't? Then what?"

Natazhia thought about her questions. After a long pause she said, "Honestly, I have no idea. We will have to talk to the others. Maybe even ask Ryker what he thinks."

"Let's go out to the kitchen. I am desperate for some coffee. Besides, I'm sure the others may be up and looking for us by now."

Racyne opened the door, and the two women walked nervously down the hall, neither wanting to run into Allen after the conversation that Natazhia had with him. As they approached the end of the hallway, they were relieved to see he had left the dayroom. Letting out a sigh, Natazhia asked Racyne, "How did you sleep last night?"

"Like a rock, once I finally got my brain to shut down."

Natazhia was relieved to talk about something other than their suspicions about Paul, Tallia, and the lead team. They sat down on stools at the kitchen island and chatted over coffee about Serenity and the boys while waiting for the other squad leaders. Byron was the first to join them, and they decided to wait until the others arrived to fill one another in, rather than repeating the conversation several times. Tristen was next and the three could hear her long before they saw her. It was hard for them not to laugh when Natazhia looked up at Racyne, who winked at her as they listened to the commotion. Tristen had a way of muttering to herself as she walked purposefully, shaking her head back and forth, and both women could picture her doing just that. Sure enough, as she rounded the corner, Tristen was cursing up a storm, head down as she made a beeline for the kitchen.

Looking up abruptly, Tristen said, "Wow, you're already here! What did I miss? Why didn't you come to get me?" She fired one question after another at them. "Did you talk to Ryker? What about Holly? And Professor? What'd they say?"

Natazhia and Racyne both let out giggles. "Relax, Tristen," Natazhia said, laughing good-naturedly, "we haven't discussed anything yet. We were waiting for you, and now for Dian."

"Oh! Good!" she exclaimed, "I didn't miss anything!" Tristen paused for a second. "But why didn't ya get me?"

The others shook their heads, and Racyne answered. "Everyone had a long day yesterday, and we didn't know how much sleep you got; I figured it best to let everyone get as much rest as they could. We may just have a bunch more in a row of long days and sleepless nights."

Satisfied with her answer, Tristen nodded slowly. "Yeah, I get that; it makes sense. Thanks, I guess."

Byron said, "Hey, I think when Dian does get here, we ought to go to that table in the dining facility again. You know, just in case."

"Okay," Racyne said in agreement. "Let's give it another fifteen minutes, and then I'll go look for Dian. Paul and Tallia should have taken the others to Base Camp by now. We shouldn't have them to worry about. It's the lead trainers I'm more concerned with now."

"It is just a hologram," Tristen said. "I mean, how much harm can they really do? It's not like they can leave or anyone can get in or out, right?"

"I don't know, Tristen," Byron said impatiently, "but I'm not interested in waiting around forever to find out! Where the hell is Dian?"

"Why don't you all go down to the dining facility?" Natazhia said. "I'll go by Dian's room and grab her, and we will meet you there."

Without waiting for a response, Natazhia headed for the hall to Dian's room. She hated to admit it, but she was beginning to feel just as impatient as Byron. Now that the others confirmed she had cause to be suspicious, she wanted to get to the bottom of it. She was tired of questioning everything and not finding any answers. For the first time in months, she felt like she might finally find the answers she was looking for.

Natazhia knocked on Dian's door loudly, forgetting that the disturbance might alert the lead trainers that the squad leaders were all together. Fortunately, Dian opened the door right away, and they disappeared back down the hall quickly toward the dining facility. When they arrived, the others were seated at the same table they'd shared the night before. The kitchen had closed a few minutes earlier, so they were alone. Natazhia quickly brought everyone up to speed on her conversations with Ryker and Professor.

"I can't believe he talked to you that way!" Tristen exclaimed after she'd shared Allen's response to her questions. "So, then the lead trainers are all in on whatever Paul and Tallia are doing, then?"

"Well, it certainly seems as though Professor is, anyway," Natazhia said. "We don't know for sure about the others. Although, I would have expected Allen to be the most loyal to Zyra Kim, especially given his maturity. I mean, he is the one most likely to have memories of what real freedom was like before the government started stripping away our rights."

"Byron," Tristen said, turning away from Natazhia, "did you talk to Holly?"

"I did. She wasn't very forthcoming, but she did tell me that she thought we should trust our instincts. I got the feeling she wanted to say more, but something is holding her back."

Racyne recapped for the group. "So basically, they've all confirmed that our suspicions are valid, but no one will disclose what's going on or what we should do about it."

Byron said, "Yes, that about sums it up."

"Didn't Paul and Tallia take the rest of the team to Base Camp this morning?" Dian asked.

Racyne said, "Yes, they were supposed to leave early."

"We should go," said Dian.

"Ryker said they had it under control," Natazhia said, objecting.

"And you believe him?" Dian pressed her to consider every angle.

Natazhia defended her husband. "Of course, I do. He wouldn't lie to me."

"Natazhia, I'm not saying he's lying," Dian said in a less argumentative tone. "We just don't know how much he truly knows. I think we need to get to the arena and find our way to Base Camp now. They took us out and made us wait for four days for a reason. I don't want to give them time to sabotage the work we did with the team a few days back."

"She's right, Natazhia," Byron said. "If they are staging a coup, they need numbers. I think our team is loyal to Zyra Kim and her vision. They can't turn them in a few hours. A few days, maybe, but not a few hours. I say we go now. They won't expect it."

Tristen said, "Dumb question here, but um, well, uh, how will we get in?"

"Leave it to Tristen to point out the obvious," said Racyne, laughing. "Byron, I think you have a point, but she's right. We have no way in, and if we are concerned about cameras seeing us talk, I seriously doubt we will get across the shelter to the arena unnoticed, especially carrying our packs."

"We don't have to go unnoticed," Byron said, countering. "We just need to get a jump start on the lead trainers and anyone else who follows. We can barricade ourselves in. We don't even need the packs."

"What do you mean we don't need the packs? The hologram also simulates the weather conditions. We will freeze!" Natazhia said, alarmed.

"Not if we shut the hologram down," Byron said smugly.

"Wait, what?" said Dian. "Do you think it's that simple? That we just shut it down?"

"Sure, why not? It's not like they are actually leaving the room. We get in, we shut it down, and we confront them."

"What if we're wrong?" Natazhia asked.

"What if we are right?" said Byron.

"Okay, you're right, but we don't have all the evidence; we don't even know for sure what they have planned," Natazhia said, musing. "Besides, you haven't said how you plan to get in."

"Oh Natazhia, how quick you forget." Byron chided her.

"Forget what?" she asked.

"We gained the ability to access the arena when we became squad leaders, remember?" Byron said.

"But if we confront them without evidence, how can we be sure we are right or that we can stop them?" said Natazhia.

"Look, Natazhia," said Byron, speaking with a new strength of conviction, "let's say we are right, we do nothing, and then Paul and Tallia stage a coup. Do you think you could live with the results knowing we had a chance to stop it?"

"You're right, Byron. But what if we're wrong?"

"What if? The way I see it, they told us Mount Everest was the final test. What if the test is to see if we will do something? So, if we are wrong, well, we just say we thought it was part of the test."

"Okay," Natazhia said, smiling at him in spite of herself, "you've got me. What do the rest of you think?"

"I'm in," Racyne said.

"Me too," said Tristen.

"I'm in," Dian said, with thumbs up.

"Great! Let's go," said Byron, standing up.

"You mean, right now?" Natazhia asked weakly.

"Yes, right now," Byron said impatiently.

What would a courageous woman do in this situation? "Okay," she said, standing up.

The others stood, and together they left the dining facility and briskly walked to the arena. When they arrived at the closed door, Byron held his bracelet up, and the door opened. Immediately the icy air blasted them. The five squad leaders filed in and pushed the door shut behind them. They quickly grabbed chairs from either side of the door and shoved them in front of it to stall anyone coming later to stop them. Looking into the arena, Natazhia could barely make out figures in the middle of the Everest hologram, confirming the remaining forty were in the simulation.

Byron took the lead. "Ready?"

They all nodded, so he lifted his wrist and said, "Mount Everest, Off," and just like that, the mountain disappeared, and the temperature warmed almost instantaneously.

Several group members looked in their direction while others looked around, somewhat disoriented by the sudden change in landscape. The evidence on the floor around the group indicated they were likely at Base Camp eating a meal, possibly on the way (or perhaps even at) the location the lead trainers and squad leaders were to meet them a few days later. They seemed to have set up a rather sophisticated camp to protect them from the simulated—yet just as harsh—weather conditions provided by the real Mount Everest.

Startled, Paul and Tallia turned with surprise to see the five squad leaders standing there.

At the same time, Natazhia looked at Byron with a questioning glance. She was unsure what to do next. They had expected to find them doing something more threatening than actually participating in the Mount Everest simulation.

Tallia soon regained her composure. "You're three days early, and why have you shut down the simulation? How can your team expect to pass the test if you shut it down before they even get to Base Camp?" Turning to Paul, she said, "We were clearly wrong about them."

Paul simply nodded.

"For a second time, you've held up the final test," said Tallia, looking derisively at the five squad leaders. "I'm beginning to think you are avoiding it. If that's the case, you've succeeded. Your actions today constitute a major breach of the trust we placed in you, and quite frankly, I don't want you on my team."

Byron immediately spoke, sounding defensive. "That's okay, Tallia, 'cause we aren't exactly interested in being on your team. We are here to be a part of Zyra Kim's mission and vision. And I don't believe you or Paul are part of her team."

The remaining forty were on their feet now, standing behind Tallia and Paul, watching as the scene unfolded. Natazhia scanned the room as her eyes adjusted to the low lighting that replaced the hologram when they shut it down. In each corner of the room stood the lead trainers. She nudged Racyne to get her attention and nodded in the direction of the corner Allen was standing in. They hadn't expected them to be there.

"That's ridiculous, Byron," Tallia said, challenging him. "Paul and I have shared the vision Zyra shared with you for many years. Long before all of you arrived and learned enough to believe you know better than us, we were students of her predecessor, Jack Kerrington. It's his vision that we are committed to and his vision that we bring to this arena. He may have left the physical operation to Zyra, but he left the mission itself in all of our hearts."

"We know you're planning a coup!" Tristen blurted out the words, unable to control herself.

Racyne grabbed Tristen's hand and gave her a stern look. Already realizing what she'd done, Tristen's face flushed bright red and she sheepishly looked down at the ground.

The lead trainers began walking toward the center of the room to join Paul and Tallia, all except Holly, who hung back at the corner closest to the door.

Tallia leaned over and whispered something to Paul. Afterward, he walked a few feet toward Professor who was heading in their direction and whispered in his ear. Professor nodded and raised his wrist and bracelet to his mouth. The alarms immediately sounded, and the familiar AI voice blared above the noise of the forty who were asking questions of each other. "Security Breach in the Training Sector. All available Security Personnel Please Report to the Training Sector."

Natazhia heard the familiar click of the security bolts opening on the door and she knew the chairs would be slowing down those on the outside of it from getting in as they tried to force it open. She looked at the other team leaders, unsure of what to do next. They hadn't discussed what they would do once they got to the arena. Then Natazhia heard Ryker's voice calling from outside the door.

"Natazhia, let us in!"

She looked at Racyne, who gave her a quick nod, and the two of them rushed over to the door and began pulling the chairs away. Behind them, Natazhia heard Byron yell.

"Stop them!"

Natazhia turned to see an opening behind the platform that she'd never noticed. Tallia and Paul were herding the others through into the dark void. Byron, Tristen, and Dian ran over to the opening and began pleading with the others. "You're making a mistake; they aren't being honest with you!"

Holly still hung back by the door, appearing hesitant to do anything, and Natazhia yelled at her.

"Dammit, Holly, you have to make a decision. Pick a side. Help us with these chairs!"

Holly came over and helped Racyne and Natazhia move the chairs. Finally, there was enough of an opening that Ryker and Grayson were able to squeeze through. They rushed in and ran across the room to the newly-revealed exit, where they grabbed Paul and Tallia by the arms.

"No one leaves!" said Grayson, his voice a growl.

Tallia and Paul were quiet and Ryker followed behind as Grayson led the pair to the chairs on the platform where they usually sat during instruction.

Satisfied that Tallia and Paul were being cooperative, Grayson looked at Ryker and said, "Follow the ones who already left, gather them up, and bring them back."

"Yes, sir," Ryker said and disappeared through the opening.

Racyne, Holly, and Natazhia cleared the remaining chairs, allowing the door to open fully just as several of Zyra's security officers appeared, followed by Zyra.

"Quiet, everyone!" Zyra said in a commanding voice. The alarms subsided, and those who had left the room began filing back in. "Find yourselves a chair and sit down. No one leaves this room until the security investigation is complete. My team will be asking—"

Tallia burst out. "Cut the crap, Zyra! Let's just be honest with them. They have a right to know they're just prisoners."

"That's an interesting perspective, Tallia. Feel free to expand." Zyra smiled.

"Do you seriously think they will remain when they find out you've kept them here, underground and away from their loved ones for no reason?"

The room filled with the buzz of the forty whispering to one another, trying to determine what Tallia meant.

"Tallia, that's where you and I differ. You see no reason to sacrifice while I see the possibility of a world that works for everyone with no one left behind, and that's worth sacrifice."

"But they didn't choose into this sacrifice, Zyra!" Tallia said, spitting with disgust. "You manipulated them through fear. You lied to them! Just like you've lied to us."

"No, Tallia! I gave them an experience. I offered them the conditions they required to become the leaders of a New World View. I created a scenario for them to experience their greatness and to push themselves to be the best they can be!"

"But you weren't honest with them, and you lied to them about the war!"

Byron stood up, red-faced and angry. "What is she talking about? What does she mean, you lied to us about the war?"

Others followed his lead, and there was a chorus of questions and demands throughout the room.

"We want answers!"

"We want the truth!"

"Tell us what's going on!"

"There were no attacks; it's been business as usual above ground since the day you arrived!" Tallia pointed at Zyra. "She lied to you to get you down here and continued to lie to keep you here!"

Natazhia looked at Zyra. "Is that true?"

She could tell by the look on Zyra's face, it was the truth.

Zyra began to justify her actions. "You wouldn't have learned what you did without believing the experience was real."

Natazhia looked at Ryker, standing at the opening with the others he'd brought back in. "Did you know?"

Ryker's face turned white.

Tears began streaming down Natazhia's face from the realization that her husband had lied to her for months. He had kept her and their children from their home and taken away their choice in the matter by not including her in the plan.

Dian said, "Natazhia, explain this to me; I don't understand."

Natazhia answered Dian while looking coldly at Zyra. "Just like Mount Everest, this whole setup has all been a simulation. Everything from the bombing that brought us here to the reports. All of it. None of it has been confirmed. We've been locked down here for months for no reason."

Zyra tried to defend herself. "Not for no reason, Natazhia. You've grown; you've become a leader of leaders, someone who will make a huge impact on this world. You wouldn't have done that without the added pressure of the simulation. Sometimes, the end justifies the means."

Racyne was sobbing behind her. "You mean all of this time, Doug's been alive?" She paused, choking on her tears and shaking her head. "You led me to believe he was dead and he's up there somewhere feeling as though I left him to die just so you could play some psychological game with us?"

"It's not like that, Racyne," Zyra said. "Listen up, everyone. I care deeply for you and all of your loved ones. We gave your loved ones the option of remaining at home for you to reunite with them or to remain in an adjoining compound. After the conclusion of Mount Everest, you would all have been reunited. Some would stay on, and others would have left. Had Paul and Tallia not chosen to attempt—" She paused and looked over at the two of them. "I'm not sure what it was that they were attempting; I'd love to hear exactly what your plan was, but later." Then, facing Racyne and the other forty, Zyra said, "Everything would have been disclosed to you at that time."

Tears still streaming down her face, Natazhia questioned Zyra's motives. "How can you say you care deeply for us and our loved ones and at the same time divide families by forcing them to lie to one another?"

"Natazhia, no one was forced to lie to anyone. Those who chose roles that allowed access to their loved ones made the choice to lie for the good of the mission. That includes your husband."

Natazhia looked at Ryker again. His head was down, and he avoided making any eye contact with her. His response hurt her even more than learning that he'd been lying to her ever since—when? Since they'd arrived at the compound? Since Zyra singled him out? Natazhia also felt incredibly foolish that she never suspected her husband of lying to her. For a moment, she remembered the beautiful words Ryker had written in the journal he gifted her, now seeing them and him in a less faithful light. Then, looking past her husband, she saw a figure at the opening. It was the clothier! He was connected!

"What are you doing here?" Natazhia cried out at the sight of him.

He grinned back at her.

It was the same look she remembered from that day at the trading post that had changed everything about her life; a pit formed in her stomach.

"I've been here all along. Who do you think orchestrated all of this?" With eyes twinkling, he said, "Zyra has much too kind of a heart to create the kind of fear and panic required to ensure every single one of you believed the simulation. If it wasn't for Paul and Tallia's interference, we would have brought it to a very successful conclusion in a few days. And still, overall, I believe it was a success!"

"A success! How can you say that?" Natazhia said in a shriek.

He chuckled. "Their interference created a sounder measurement of our test than the Mount Everest experience ever could have done. As the unintended result, we have discovered which leaders are truly loyal to the mission. We've witnessed those who are willing to trust their intuition and take a stand the way your friends have done. And we've been able to identify those who would turn away without even questioning what the truth might be. Yes, I do believe that ultimately our New World will win as a result of all that has transpired in these inal few days. That is, provided those of you who have displayed true servant leadership look past what was not disclosed to you from the start and understand that, in the end, you and those you care about benefitted. Remember, every choice has prices and benefits. Zyra made choices. Your loved ones made choices, and you made the choice to be here. Everyone paid prices and everyone received benefits."

Natazhia sat back down and took a deep breath, contemplating all that he had said. The others must have been chewing on his diatribe as well. She wanted nothing more than to get out of that room, find her children, and leave. She wanted to go home with her children, and she wasn't sure if she even wanted her husband to go with them. *How could he have kept this from me? When did he first know?* Natazhia didn't know how to feel. Anger, fear, and betrayal all made sense, yet none of those emotions described the numbness that consumed her.

After listening to the clothier, who had occupied her thoughts for months and left more questions than answers, she had to admit that he might have done more good than harm. *But is it justifiable to go to such lengths for the greater good?* She was grateful for the person she had become. She appreciated her new friendships. She had experienced what life might be like someday when she didn't have to hide the twins from society. Natazhia looked at the inside of her wrist and gazed at the washed-out, pale color of the stone. She knew that it wasn't the time for her to make a decision.

PREVIEW OF THE SEQUEL

Natazhia stood just inside the gate after ducking through the overgrown thorny blackberry bushes to step into the familiar scene of home ground. A stinging sensation on her forearm drew her gaze to the olive fabric of her uniform where she'd torn it on the thorns, revealing a fresh cut. She carefully closed and locked the gate behind her and took a deep breath in the dry heat of the afternoon sun. Then, braced for the worst, she surveyed the property. Scanning the landscape, Natazhia felt a mixture of relief to return from months underground and high alert when she heard a rustling sound from behind the garden. Instinctively, she reached for her Browning .380 strapped to her leg. More than a self-defense weapon, it had been a gift left behind by her late mother. She was grateful for its return when she checked out of the compound earlier that morning. Cautiously side-stepping around the garden to determine the source of the noise, then laughing as her eyes teared up, she lowered the gun. The family's goat, Hattie, was grazing on the shaded grass below the overgrowth from months of neglect.

"Hattie," she called as the goat looked up, startled, pausing mid-munch and then bleating and running toward her. Natazhia squatted down and scratched the goat on its neck. "Oh, my goodness, girl! I can't believe you're still here." She looked around, bewildered that the property had sustained her family pet. Then, standing up, with the goat bleating as she followed behind, Natazhia began searching for Agatha, the egg-producer, wondering if she might have also survived.

ABOUT THE AUTHOR

Brenda Kilhoffer is an "Army Brat" turned Air Force Veteran. Growing up as the daughter and granddaughter of a traditional military family, knowing nothing else, in 1988, she enlisted in the Air Force. Then in 1994, she left everything she knew behind and moved to Arizona to change the trajectory of her life. Her training led to a corporate career with the phone company. Ever adaptable and open to challenges, Brenda pursued a career in Real Estate, which led to her discovering the world of personal and professional development.

Having found her passion, Brenda began coaching, writing, and speaking. She builds communities of like-minded people and has helped hundreds break through limiting beliefs and go on to create success for themselves. She's passionate about freedom, leadership, and personal development. She believes that every human being has inner genius. She aims to reveal the genius in others by demonstrating how to conquer limiting beliefs and inspiring them to step into purpose! Brenda is a hard-working and driven visionary with demonstrated success in Corporate America, Real Estate, Entrepreneurship, and as a Speaker and Best-Selling Author. Outside of her work-passion, she enjoys horseback riding and tending to the animals on her small two-acre hobby farm.

Family time includes the love and care of horses, cows, chickens, turkeys, ducks, dogs, and cats alongside her husband, Rodney, and their children—Jaelyn, Jacob, and Jeremiah, with frequent visits from their oldest son, Jordan, daughter-in-love, Lexi, and grandson, Eli.

Connect with Brenda

https://linktr.ee/cheapmama
Brenda@CheapMamaLife.com
https://www.linkedin.com/in/cheapmama/

We LOVE Reviews.
We invite you to leave a review on
Amazon and Goodreads.

If you would like to be informed when Brenda's next book is released, please connect with her here:
www.CheapMamaLife.com